EVERYONE ON BOARD THE *JACQUELINE* HAD THE OPPORTUNITY. TOO MANY HAD THE MOTIVE . . .

MOLLY HUBBARD O'CONNOR: Sweet and cheerful, she waited on Poppa hand and foot. After his unwelcome dip in the canal, she finally convinced him to write a will, leaving his estate in equal thirds to her children, and to his son Michel whom he had never seen . . .

ELLEN AND DON HUBBARD: Poppa O'Connor had never adopted his stepchildren—or given Don the partnership in the agency he so clearly deserved. But it was Ellen, whose computer career had taken her out of Poppa's suffocating grasp, who resented him most . . .

ROSANNA ROSSI AND TONIO RICCARDI: The celebrated opera diva had been with Poppa so long she was like family. She was delighted that her handsome young lover would sing the lead in *La Bohème*—and furious that Poppa would not get her the role of his leading lady . . .

KURT GEBLER AND JULIE BERGSTROM: Poppa's latest protégé played the violin with fabulous precision . . . yet it was his accompanist who had the true soul of a musician. But Julie had refused to sign with O'Connor Enterprises . . .

CAPTAIN EMILE MICHEL ARNAUD AND MARIE DUPONT: The pretty stewardess was sleeping in Emile's cabin, but at every stop along the canal she was seen talking with a mysterious young man on a motorcycle. Like Kurt and Tonio, Emile was the right age to be Poppa's son—and his rough treatment of Marie proved his capacity for violence . . .

MURDER IN BURGUNDY

Audrey Peterson

POCKET BOOKS

New York   London   Toronto   Sydney   Tokyo

An *Original* Publication of POCKET BOOKS

POCKET BOOKS, a division of Simon & Schuster Inc.
1230 Avenue of the Americas, New York, NY 10020

ISBN: 0-671-65737-2

First Pocket Books printing December 1989

10 9 8 7 6 5 4 3 2 1

POCKET and colophon are trademarks of
Simon & Schuster Inc.

Printed in the U.S.A.

For Jacqueline

With grateful acknowledgment to Floating Through Europe, Inc., whose delightful crew members bear no resemblance to some of those in the book.

MURDER IN BURGUNDY

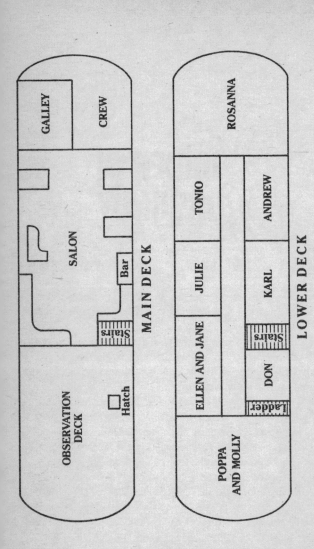

GALLEY

CREW

SALON

Bar

Stairs

MAIN DECK

OBSERVATION
DECK

Hatch

ROSANNA

TONIO

ANDREW

JULIE

KARL

ELLEN AND JANE

DON

Stairs

POPPA
AND MOLLY

Ladder

LOWER DECK

The *Jacqueline*

1

knew I shouldn't have let you out of my sight, Jane."

It was my husband, James, speaking. I looked into those blue blue eyes and smiled. "I'll be gone only a week or so."

"Yes, but you're just back from California, and now you're off to France in a few days. For a bride of six months, you seem to be taking a somewhat cavalier attitude toward your wifely duties."

It was the first week in June and the afternoon sun, coming through the window, was doing its watery best to pretend it was summer. Sitting on the sofa in our London flat, we were finishing the last of a bottle of Chardonnay I had brought from Los Angeles. At least James was sitting. I was stretched out with my bare feet in his lap while he idly massaged my toes.

"Wifely duties, indeed! Now that I can be addressed as 'Dr. Winfield,' I expect to be treated with more respect."

For the past two years I had been in London,

finishing my doctoral dissertation in music history, and had just returned from my university in Los Angeles, where I had given the oral defense, presided over by my professor, Dr. Andrew Quentin.

James gave me a look of mock reproof. "I should have known you and Andrew would cook up something between you. Last year you two were involved in a murder. You'd best keep your eyes open on this hotel barge and try not to trip over dead bodies."

I giggled. "Yes, darling, I promise. It's only a small group—the O'Connor family and some of Poppa O'Connor's clients. It's true that my friend Ellen might decide to murder her stepfather, but she's hated him for so many years, there's no reason why she should suddenly take to mayhem on a family holiday."

"So when do you leave for Paris?"

"They've booked a flight for me out of Heathrow on Saturday afternoon. Look, darling, couldn't you possibly get away and come along? Now that you're Hall, Smith, Dexter, and Hall, you should have more freedom."

James had recently been made a full partner in the firm of solicitors in which his father, before his death, had been the first Hall.

He tweaked one of my toes. "Don't I wish I could! I'm booked to the eyebrows for the next two months, but I'm hanging on to our August holiday for dear life. No, you go along, love. Maybe you can find a wife for Andrew and then we can all wallow in domesticity."

"Poor lamb—how you suffer! Speaking of domesticity, if I were a proper wife, I'd be fixing a meal instead of lollygagging about like this."

Thoughtfully, James selected another toe, bending over to nibble it lightly. "So much for the hors d'oeuvres," he murmured. Picking up his glass, he swallowed the last of his wine. "I'm in no hurry for dinner. It seems to me there's a good deal to be said for lollygagging."

This is the point at which old-fashioned authors used to put a row of asterisks. I need only say that we did dine eventually, going around the corner to our favorite brasserie. James is the least demanding of husbands, which is fortunate, since I adore good food but would much rather let someone else prepare it.

What happened in France in the following week went to prove that one should never joke about death. There was trouble brewing on several fronts but nothing that I would have thought would lead to such tragic consequences. We were scheduled to gather in Paris on Saturday at the Hotel Meurice, where the O'Connors, who never did things by halves, were picking up the tab for all their guests. The party included my friend Ellen and her brother Don, my professor, Andrew Quentin, and some musicians who were clients of O'Connor Enterprises, one of the top talent agencies in the United States, which was run by "Poppa" O'Connor, Ellen's stepfather.

"Rosanna's coming," Ellen had told me, referring to the celebrated diva, Rosanna Rossi. "She's bringing a tenor who's her current protégé. And Poppa's invited Karl Gebler, some young violinist he's very keen on just now. He and the girl who is his accompanist are doing a recital in Paris the night before we leave for the boat."

Ellen and I had been friends since undergraduate days at the University of California at Berkeley. We were both from Los Angeles and had continued to see a lot of each other in the following few years. While I went on to graduate studies in music, I lived at home with my father, having lost my mother at the age of twelve. Ellen also lived at home for a time while getting started in computer programming and was now a free-lance consultant. Her marriage to a Los Angeles lawyer had started out well but was just now ending in a divorce that was mutually agreed upon but not without pain.

When I told her I hoped the week on the cruise would be good for her, she simply rolled her eyes and said that a week at close quarters with Poppa was not her idea of therapy, but she had promised her mother she'd go.

It was hard for me to judge whether or not Poppa O'Connor was really as bad as Ellen made out. On the many occasions before Ellen's marriage when I had visited her at their palatial home in the Hollywood Hills, he had always been cordial to me—"My name's Michael, but call me Poppa, everyone does"—but I had to admit that there could be something phony behind all that charm, although I couldn't say exactly what it was. Ellen's mother, Molly, was a genuine darling. A short, plump woman with lovely brown eyes and a sweet smile, she had been widowed when her children were very young—Ellen two and Don just four—and had married Poppa O'Connor two years later.

"Poppa was never the cruel stepfather," Ellen had told me. "He just didn't care that much about us. I remember climbing up in his lap, and he would sort of pat me absentmindedly and go on talking. Then he'd say, 'Run along now, Ellen,' and I knew he was bored with me. And of course he was always totally involved in the business."

I knew the basic facts of Poppa's career. He was the kind of self-made man who made Horatio Alger look tame. Starting in New York City in his early twenties with a few bookings for singers and dancers, he rose through boundless energy and sheer good luck to a position in which many of the world's greatest musicians were his clients. In the early years he had sought out those with promising talent and relentlessly scrounged bookings for them. Ultimately the balance shifted, and those on the way up often sought out his agency. To be represented by O'Connor Enterprises became a distinction and sometimes a ticket to fame and fortune, especially, I gathered, if the artist stayed on the good side of Poppa.

Now I was about to learn a good deal more about Poppa's life, because Andrew Quentin and I were commissioned to write his biography. It all came about when Ellen called me in Los Angeles on my recent visit there.

"Poppa's all excited," she said. "Some literary agent called and said they're interested in publishing the story of his life and asked if he knows someone to do it. He said to ask you to recommend someone, Jane. They want a published name, someone with prestige."

I thought of my professor and promised to ask him. Although only in his thirties, Andrew had already published two books and a number of scholarly articles, so he would have the "name," but I wasn't sure he would want to do something in the commercial field. When I called him, he said he needed a break from his usual stuff and he wouldn't mind making some extra money. Then he surprised me by saying that he would consider it only if I would collaborate with him. The project was too much for him to handle alone, what with teaching and his other research in hand, but with my help he could work it out.

The agent then brought us together with Poppa and the publisher's representative and in due course we signed a contract. That was when Poppa invited us to come along on the canal cruise in Burgundy.

"There'll be hours to kill on that boat," he said. "I don't know how I let Molly talk me into this, but it looks like we're really going. So you two can interview me there!"

2

On the following Saturday afternoon, I arrived at the elegant Meurice, feeling somewhat like Cinderella at the ball. As a solicitor, James had an income that was more than adequate but in no way in the Meurice class. A modest hotel on the Left Bank was more our style for Paris. I was happy to see that my room, with its rich fabrics and glowing wood, had not been converted to trendy modern but still retained an Old World elegance.

At a few minutes before five I went down to the cocktail lounge to meet Ellen.

"Don's coming in from Los Angeles—he should be here soon," she said, her green eyes smiling. I knew how much she adored her brother. Our drinks had just arrived when we saw Don coming toward us.

"Hi, sis! Hi, Jane!" He hugged each of us in turn and collapsed into a low chair.

Ellen smiled at him, pushing the fair hair back from her forehead. "So, how was your flight?"

"Right on time for once. I took a taxi from de

Gaulle. Saturday afternoon the traffic's not bad. I got your note, popped up to my room, and here I am—not even five o'clock. Pretty good, huh?''

Don, with his dark hair and his mother Molly's brown eyes, did not seem at first glance to resemble his sister. Upon closer examination, however, one saw the family likeness in the cast of their features.

Don looked at our glasses. ''I see Jane has wine. What's yours, Ellen?''

''A cassis.''

He grinned. ''Not for me. Too sweet.'' To the waiter who had appeared, he said, ''Whisky soda, *s'il vous plaît.*''

''So, sis, how was Italy?''

''Heavenly, as always.'' Ellen held out her left hand. ''I bought this in Florence.''

Don took her hand and studied the ring of little sapphires and diamonds in a simple but elegant setting. ''In place of the wedding ring?'' he asked.

''Yes.'' His sister's green eyes looked steadily into his. ''The divorce will be final in a few months, you know. It's time to move on.''

Don looked at her with concern. ''Ellie, are you okay?''

''Yes, darling, really okay.''

Turning to me, Don asked, ''How's James?''

''Thriving!'' I replied.

Ellen laughed. ''Look at that glowing face, Don. I'd say it's love, wouldn't you?''

One of the great things about Ellen was that even though her own marriage had foundered, she took genuine pleasure in my happiness with James.

Ellen looked at her brother. ''How are things at home?''

''Oh, the usual minor hassles at the office. But Harry keeps the lid on things, thank God. So, Ellie—

18

what do you think of Poppa really going through with this cruise?"

"I know what you mean. He never takes a real vacation. I suppose once they had chartered the boat for the week he couldn't very well back out. Besides, Momma put the pressure on. With Poppa's heart problems, she's been insisting he get some rest."

Don looked at me. "You know, Jane, the sad thing is that Harry and I can handle the business perfectly well without him, but he thinks O'Connor Enterprises would go down the drain if he isn't there every minute. The staff have no more than the usual crises, and now that we are set up with the computer—thanks to Ellen—we've got everything humming. Of course the talent are always temperamental. I have to admit that that's Poppa's forte. When he turns on the charm, they do respond."

Ellen said, "This trip must be costing him a packet."

"It is, but Poppa can afford it. It's making a slight dent in the assets but not enough to notice."

"You should know, Don. You write the bills."

"And a good thing too. Poppa needs a steady hand."

"So, Don, tell us more about who's coming on this cruise. During my two weeks in Italy I haven't kept up with the latest."

Don grinned. "Well, it started out to be just the family, but you know Poppa—he has to have a crowd around or he isn't happy. So next we get Rosanna—she's been around so long she's practically a member of the family anyway—and her current acquisition. He's a tenor named Tonio Riccardi. We're representing him, by the way, and he's really good."

Ellen laughed. "Hardly dry behind the ears, if I know Rosanna."

"You're so right. Somewhere in his twenties. Just about half her age, I would guess. They get younger as she gets older, a sort of inverse ratio."

"And who's the violinist?"

"It's a young fellow named Karl Gebler. He won the Silver Medal at the Levenstein competition and we signed him up right away. He had offers from other agencies, but he chose us. When we were doing the contract, he positively fawned over Poppa and needless to say Poppa fell for him like a ton of bricks. When Poppa found out that Gebler had two recitals this week over here—one in Paris tonight and another in Lyons on Wednesday—he insisted that he come with us on the barge, along with his accompanist."

"I'm glad plenty of people are coming. It will keep Poppa happy."

When our drinks were finished, Ellen stood up and stretched. "Anyone for a walk?"

The three of us sauntered out of the hotel. A shower earlier that day had cleared away, and the sun splashed shadows along the Rue de Rivoli as we strolled along under the arcade, looking idly into the windows of the little shops. At the Place de la Concorde we turned toward the river.

The trees along the Seine were lushly green. Ellen looked up, smiling, her fair hair dappled by the shadows of the leaves. "How I love really leafy trees. Southern California is great, but can eucalyptus trees and those silly date palms ever compete with anything like this?"

I laughed. "I agree. But not many cities can compete with Paris, anyway." We looked down the long side of the Louvre on our left and at the marvelous old buildings across the river.

Don nodded, then yawned. "Jane, I hear you and Andrew are going to the Gebler recital tonight. I'm glad I don't have to go. After that flight I need some sleep."

Ellen asked, "Does anyone *have* to go?"

"Well, not really. But since we are here, Poppa thought someone should turn up."

"Don't worry, Don," I said. "I'm looking forward to it."

Presently we stopped to lean on the wall above the quay and watch the traffic on the river. Don broke the silence. "Thank God Momma's all right. A year ago we were all pretty scared."

In the spring of the preceding year Molly had had a mastectomy but had made an excellent recovery.

Ellen's eyes followed a sight-seeing boat as it moved along under its gaily striped awning. "Momma is the reason I came on this trip, actually. I wouldn't have come for Poppa, but when Dr. McLaren told Momma everything was clear—no sign of cancer—I knew this week on the boat meant a real celebration for her."

"Don't be too hard on Poppa, Ellie. He's okay—well, most of the time, anyway."

"Oh, Don, you're an angel to put up with him. I wish I had your patience. Remember when we were little and Momma was always after him to adopt us? We weren't supposed to know, but I could hear them arguing and I used to cry because I wanted him to be my real daddy."

Don turned to me. "Yes, it was harder for Ellen because she was too little to remember our own father. Not that I remembered him very well—I was barely four when he died. Still, I didn't mind not being adopted because I thought our own daddy was up in heaven looking down and he might not like it."

I noticed Ellen didn't smile at this childish fancy. Instead, her mouth tightened.

"Anyhow," she said, "I'm glad now that Poppa

didn't do the adoption. This way I don't have to feel guilty that we don't get along. Sometimes when he turns on that phony charm I feel—well, a kind of senseless fury. I just want to—'' Her fists clenched. Then she laughed. ''Sometimes I think I'd kill him if I thought I could get away with it!''

3

That evening I went with Andrew Quentin to the recital given by the O'Connor protégé, Karl Gebler. We had decided on evening dress, and I wore one of my favorites from my trousseau, a pale yellow gown which James regarded as suitably sexy but proper. Andrew in black tie was looking dazzling and, as usual, quite unaware of his attractiveness. The right girl would surely come along one of these days, I thought. Since the death of his young wife, he had withdrawn into a private world of grief which never seemed to affect his professional life, but which I knew had left him emotionally scarred.

We stopped along the way for a quick meal at one of those little Paris cafés where a bowl of soup and a piece of fish emerge as small masterpieces of culinary art.

"How on earth do the French do it?" I murmured. "Much as I adore living in England, I have to admit their way with food is deplorable. Tasteless peas pressed onto the back of the fork with equally tasteless mashed potatoes seem perfectly acceptable to the average Englishman.''

Andrew smiled. "You sound like Norma!"

I nearly swallowed a fish bone in my surprise. Although we had become good friends during the two years he had supervised my dissertation, he had rarely spoken to me of his wife.

Now he went on, his sensitive face alight with recollection. "She loved good food, especially here in Paris. There was a little place not far from here we used to like. I thought of going there tonight, Jane, but"—he looked at me almost apologetically—"I wasn't sure I was quite ready for it.''

I tried to keep my voice steady. "Yes, I understand." What if something happened to James, I thought. Oh, dear God, how could I bear it?

"It was all so totally unexpected," Andrew went on. "Perhaps if there had been a long illness—some sort of warning—''

"It was a car accident, wasn't it?"

"Yes. She went out to mail a letter. I offered to take it for her the next morning, but it was the end of a stifling day and a breeze had come up. She said, 'No, I'll just walk down to the box. The cool air will feel good.' ''

Andrew sat staring at his wineglass, and I said nothing to break the spell. Then his quiet voice continued. "It was quite senseless. She crossed the street and had nearly reached the curb when a car spun around the corner at high speed. A fifteen-year-old boy had taken the keys to the family car, piled in his friends, and set off to get some ice cream. They weren't drinking or on drugs. The boy who was driving was just being silly, showing off. Evidently he had said to the other kids, 'Wanna see me take a corner on two wheels?'

"Norma was thrown thirty feet. By the time she reached the hospital she was in a coma and a few hours later she was gone."

How often I had seen that look of pain cross Andrew's face, only to be quickly banished. His tone was not one of complaint, not even of self-pity. It was one of sheer astonishment that such an oddly devastating thing could happen with no warning, making no sense. It had been nearly three years since his wife's death but I knew that at that moment it was as fresh to him as if it had been yesterday.

I said nothing, since no ordinary phrases would suit, but I felt that in some indefinable way, apart from the recent completion of my doctoral degree, this moment of confidence had ended the student-professor relationship in which we had stood for so long and marked the beginning of our friendship as equals in the scholarly profession we shared.

Reverting to his normal tone, Andrew said, "I'm looking forward to seeing my friend, Bernard Moreau. When we come to the end of the cruise in Lyon, I've planned to spend a night with him and his family. He is a member of the Police Judiciaire, which I understand is the detective branch of the Police Nationale. As a detective inspector, he works major crimes in the area."

"Did you meet your friend here in France?"

"No, actually we met in Los Angeles two years ago. Moreau was visiting his cousin, who is on the faculty in the French department at the university. Moreau is extremely fond of music, and his cousin, who declared himself a musical illiterate, called me to the rescue. Moreau and I took in all the local offerings and became good friends."

I laughed, not knowing then how prophetic my words would be. "James warned me not to trip over bodies, Andrew. Your friend might be called in if we have any murders on the canal cruise!''

When we arrived at the concert hall, we noticed with pleasure that there was a good attendance for the young artist and his pianist, who were not yet big names on the concert circuit. Presently the lights were lowered, the rustle of programs and the murmur of voices ceased, and in the hush the two young performers walked out onto the stage, bowing gracefully in unison.

Karl Gebler was slender, with dark hair and eyes so intense that he seemed to face the world with a permanent scowl. The young woman was stunning. I glanced down at my program again to look for her name—Julie Bergstrom. As she took her place at the piano, got up to turn the knob to raise the seat to a comfortable height, and pushed back the thick brown hair which was held by a band and fell loosely to her shoulders, I saw the perfection of her profile and the attractive curves of her body as she deftly shifted her long skirt to free her feet for the pedals. Meanwhile the page-turner had emerged from the wings, placed the music on the piano, and taken his seat upstage at her left while she struck the A for the violinist to tune.

Gebler raised his violin, checked his A string with the piano, and sounded the other intervals, making a slight adjustment to his E string. Then he looked toward the girl at the piano, nodded, and the recital began.

He tossed off the three short sonatas by Mozart with which the program began, exhibiting a nice precision that I had to admire. There was none of the sloppy sentimentality with which Mozart was sometimes butchered. Yet, to my taste, the pianist, Julie

Bergstrom, showed more attention to nuance, more sensitivity to the subtleties of the music, than did Gebler. Perhaps he isn't warmed up yet, I thought.

In the Beethoven which followed—a late sonata, Opus 96—Karl's formidable technique began to emerge, and in the works of Ravel and Milhaud—someone had had the good sense to include French composers on a Paris program—he displayed every accomplishment of the virtuoso from impeccable double stops to flawless harmonics.

It's an impressive talent, I thought. Yet for me that final dimension was missing in Karl's performance, that indefinable quality which could only be called a feeling for the music itself. Gebler's gestures were appropriate—he had a fine flair for body movements which were dramatic without being excessive. He could certainly make the violin sing when it was required, although I felt that the lyric passages were not his forte. Yet for me it was Julie Bergstrom at the piano who had the qualities I didn't find in Gebler.

The program ended with some Kreisler show pieces, which Gebler clearly enjoyed, and another Kreisler was done as an encore.

When the pair had returned backstage after their final bow, Andrew and I introduced ourselves, then stood aside while a handful of assorted well-wishers offered their congratulations. I noted that in addition to his native German, Karl was fluent in both French and English, although the English was accented. Julie managed a very respectable French, but her American origin was easily detected when she spoke.

When the others had gone, Andrew held out a hand to each. "You were both absolutely splendid."

"Thank you so much," Karl said in a tone that implied the accolade was principally his to accept.

27

"You selected an interesting program," I remarked.

"Oh, it was my coach who named the program," Karl tossed his head. "I like the other works all right, but I think the Mozarts are boring."

Andrew's brows shot up and I saw him steal a glance at Julie Bergstrom, but she was looking down and made no response.

Andrew changed the subject. "I enjoyed the Beethoven. I am always surprised at the sense of joy in much of the late work. It doesn't fit somehow with our picture of the aged Beethoven as the deaf and wounded lion retreating to his den."

Now Julie looked at Andrew in surprise and murmured, "Yes, how true!"

Karl looked puzzled. "Yes, I suppose so. I would rather have done the Kreutzer Sonata, but the coach said it is too often done."

Andrew said, "Yes, it offers a more spectacular role for the violin, doesn't it?" He did not smile, and Gebler, unaware of the hint of irony, agreed.

I said, "Mr. O'Connor suggested that we bring you both back to the hotel in a taxi when you are ready. Do you want to stop for food or drink along the way?"

Karl hesitated. "I would like to walk, if you don't mind. But not with the violin. Julie, will you go along and take this back with you?" It sounded more like an order than a question.

Karl loosened the bow and reverently laid bow and violin in the case, covering the strings with a cloth. "I trust you to take care," he said to Julie in the manner of a mother entrusting her infant to a nanny, and with a quick good-night he was gone.

Julie looked at us in surprise, revealing the full

beauty of her eyes, the deep blue shading to purple in the dim light in which we stood.

"Walk?" she said with a slight shrug. "I've never known Karl to walk ten feet if he could ride instead."

She picked up her coat and Karl's violin and walked rapidly toward the stage exit, calling *bon soir* to the doorman. At the top of the short flight of steps down to the street, Andrew took the violin from her and waited while she lifted her long skirt to descend. As I stood behind her, I caught sight of a figure at the street corner hailing a taxi and saw that it was Karl Gebler, who leapt in and was borne off into the night. So much for his desire for a walk. No need to mention this to Julie, I thought. She was looking down at the steps and could not have seen Karl. I wondered if they were lovers. If so, telling Julie would only cause trouble between them.

In the taxi back to the Meurice, Julie and I took the rear seat, with Andrew on the fold-out seat facing us. His first remark confirmed to me that he felt as I did about the young performers we had just heard, as he said to Julie, "You are a truly fine musician. I'm enough of an amateur pianist myself to know a good one when I hear one."

Julie looked at him, those beautiful eyes solemn. "It's good to hear that, Dr. Quentin. Karl usually gets all the tributes. Of course people say to me, 'Wonderful! Marvelous!' because I'm standing there and they must say something, but Karl is always the center of attention."

I smiled at her. "Don't be too sure they're only being polite. I agree with Andrew—you have a special quality not all musicians have."

Now the serious regard was turned to me. "Thank you! Do I call you Dr. Winfield or—er—Mrs. Hall?"

Evidently she had been clued in by someone—probably Molly—about my plethora of names. I laughed and said, "I'm not sure myself! I'm still Jane Winfield professionally, and Mrs. Hall in private life. But please, just Jane."

"And I'm Andrew, by the way." Leaning forward, his long legs folded awkwardly under the jump seat, Andrew said, "It occurs to me that one reason Gebler as the violinist gets the lion's share of attention is that most people don't understand the equal role of the piano and the violin, especially in the sonata literature. They tend to think of the violinist as the soloist and the piano as mere accompaniment, whereas Beethoven, for example, thinks of the two-instrument sonata as chamber music, with the parts balanced as they are in a trio or a quartet."

"Exactly," I added. "So the public treats the violinist as the star of the show."

Julie smiled wryly. "And Karl doesn't mind that in the least!"

"He is a bit of a showman," I said cautiously, "but that will no doubt be good for his career."

Suddenly Julie fell silent, staring out of the window of the taxi. Then she turned to both of us with what seemed at the time to be an abrupt change of subject. "How well do you know Mr. O'Connor?" she asked. It was only later on that we learned the linked train of her thought.

Andrew mentioned his brief acquaintance with O'Connor through the negotiations for the book, while I explained that I had known him casually for some years as my friend Ellen's stepfather.

Julie looked thoughtful. "Someone like Mr. O'Connor has a great deal of power, hasn't he?"

At that moment we arrived at the hotel, and while

Andrew was paying the driver, I said to Julie, "I hope you'll enjoy the cruise this week."

To my surprise, I saw her shudder, her whole body trembling. "I shouldn't have come," she said softly. "I really shouldn't have come." And with a swift "Good-night and thank-you!" she seized Karl's violin and disappeared into the hotel.

4

As Andrew and I walked down the corridor on the fourth floor of the Meurice, we turned a corner in time to see a man and a woman in a doorway engaged in a passionate kiss. As the woman came up for air, we both recognized her as Rosanna Rossi, the celebrated soprano whose face was almost as familiar to the world as that of a pop star's. Her face showing the slightly ravaged beauty of ripe middle age, she gazed adorringly at the young man whose arms embraced her plump shoulders.

The young man, turning to cross the passage to his own room, smiled deprecatingly as he saw us approach, but the great diva, totally unembarrassed by our presence, stood in her doorway blowing him kisses with all the grace of an operatic heroine saying farewell to her lover.

When her door had closed, Andrew murmured, "Mimi and Rodolfo?"

I giggled. "I was thinking of Violetta and Alfredo."

Suddenly I felt a slight grimace of pain for Andrew,

whose life at the moment held no Mimi or Violetta. As we reached my door, Andrew surprised me for the second time that evening. Clearly he had read my thoughts, for, taking my hand, he said gently, "Don't worry about me, Jane. I'm really quite all right." Then he bent down, kissed my cheek, and went off down the corridor.

Half an hour later, a minor bombshell exploded, metaphorically speaking, although none of us recognized its far-reaching consequences at the time. Ellen and I had adjoining rooms, next to her parents' suite, and I had promised her to come in for a bedtime chat. Her mother, Molly, came in to join us, and the three of us sat curled up in our nightgowns and robes, sipping cocoa.

Molly's soft brown eyes glowed as she reported that Poppa was behaving like an angel about taking the week's cruise. "I was afraid he would balk at the last moment, but he's actually promised to rest every day and follow the doctor's orders. Of course, he has already talked to Harry on the phone to check up on the Los Angeles headquarters, and he's arranged to have a phone hookup from the boat each day so he can 'keep in touch,' as he puts it. But otherwise he's being good as gold. He told me that turning seventy last month has made him think about taking things easy for a change."

As if on cue, a knock at the door revealed Poppa O'Connor himself, in pajamas and robe, in the doorway of Ellen's room.

Molly took his arm and closed the door behind him. "What is it, dear? What's happened?"

"I've just had a phone call. I can't believe it. It's just—well—it's a shock, that's all."

Poppa plopped into a chair, pulling his bathrobe over his knees and staring at Molly, his eyes round with astonishment. Everything about Poppa was round: the short plump body, the round eyes in a round Irish face, and the crown of white hair circling the bald top of his head.

"So who was the phone call from, dear?" Molly asked.

I stood up, saying, "I must be going," and started for the door, when Poppa said, "No, Jane, sit down, sit down. It's no secret."

I knew he meant it, for Poppa was one of those people with no inhibitions. In fact, I had told Andrew that Poppa would be a great subject for the biography because he didn't know the meaning of reticence.

"You'll never believe this, Doll. It was Odette."

"Odette! Good grief—after all these years!"

Ellen looked puzzled. "Who's Odette?"

Molly said placidly, "She was Poppa's first wife, dear. You remember he was married before to a French lady."

"Oh, yes, I'd forgotten. I don't know that I ever heard her name."

"No, probably not. So, Poppa, what did she want?"

"Well, she didn't exactly want anything. She just said she wanted to tell me something she had never told anyone before. It seems she was pregnant when she left me. She got that quickie divorce and went back to France and told everyone that her husband in America had died."

"How did she know you were here in Paris?"

"She saw an item in the newspaper. It was mainly about Rosanna—you know, great soprano arrives in Paris and will spend week on boat chartered by her agent, Michael O'Connor, etc. etc. It said the party was staying here at the Meurice before going to Dijon tomorrow, so she decided to give me a call."

34

"Why didn't she tell you years ago when she found out she was pregnant?"

Poppa looked sheepish. "She was pretty fed up with me when she left. Said she never wanted to see me again and all that. I had given her plenty of money as part of the divorce so she was okay in that way. She said she met this guy over here who was crazy about her and they got married soon after the baby was born. It seems she didn't want him to know she was divorced, and since he made good money, she didn't need anything from me. He died a couple of years ago and never knew that she wasn't a widow when he married her."

"Is she in need of money?"

"I guess not. At least, she didn't ask for any money—just wanted me to know. That's what I can't get over—that I'm a father. All those years when I hoped that you and I might have one of our own, Doll—and to think that all the time I was a father and didn't know it!"

Poppa's round face creased with satisfaction. "I asked her what she named the kid and she said Michel. That's French for Michael, you know."

"Yes, dear, I know."

"I knew that right away," Poppa said proudly. "You remember that French cellist we had named Michel Dupuis? He told me we had the same first name." Poppa, who I knew had no gift for languages, was obviously delighted with this evidence of his mastery of French.

Ellen spoke for the first time. "I'm surprised that Odette would name the child after you when she was so bitter toward you."

Poppa snorted. "You didn't know Odette. She was really wild and crazy. Raging and screaming one minute, sweet as pie the next. And a weird sense of humor. She probably thought it was a great joke that I had a kid with my name and never knew it."

"How old would he be now?"

Poppa frowned. "How long have we been married, Doll?"

Molly didn't bother to reproach him for not knowing. We all knew Poppa never remembered dates. She smiled gently.

"It will be twenty-four years in October."

"Okay. So it was a couple of years before that when Odette left. So the kid would be about what—about twenty-five, I guess."

"You'll want to see him, of course, won't you? Where are they living?"

"That's the maddening part. I asked Odette that and she said never mind, she would get in touch with me when we get back next week. She asked if we would be back here at the Meurice and when I said we would, she just laughed and said, 'I will call you then,' and hung up."

"Do you know what her name is now?"

"No. She didn't tell me and I've never heard a word from her from the day she left until tonight. If she doesn't call, I don't know how to find her."

"Oh, dear. Then we'll just have to wait until we return. I'm sure she'll call again next Saturday and then you can arrange to meet your other son."

"What do you mean, other son? Oh, I see, you mean Don. Well, of course, he is like my son in a way." Poppa thrust out his chest. "But, after all, it's different, isn't it, if it's your very own child?"

I saw Ellen stiffen, and when Poppa and Molly left, I wasn't surprised at her explosion.

"You heard that, Jane? He has only one son. Oh, of course Don is like a son 'in a way'! I ask you, have you ever heard anything so insensitive? Don has always been so good to Poppa, and now he virtually runs the business and still manages to make Poppa feel he's in charge. Whoever this French son is, he could never be better to him than Don has been. How can Poppa be that way?"

I thought for a moment. "It's ego, isn't it? He must have someone who is a reflection of himself."

"Yes, exactly. No wonder this Odette left him. Only an angel like Momma could ever put up with him!"

And I saw what she meant.

5

After breakfast the next morning—Sunday—we all drifted down to the lobby of the Meurice from where we were to be transported to Dijon for the start of the cruise. Poppa was in his element, playing the genial host, while Molly quietly introduced the members of the party who had not already met.

When Andrew and Don had exchanged greetings, I introduced Andrew to Ellen, noting his look of admiration as Ellen said to him, her green eyes sparkling, "I'm fascinated that someone wants to do a book on Poppa. Needless to say, he's absolutely thrilled at the prospect."

Andrew smiled. "I suppose most people are. It's a pretty flattering form of recognition for any sort of career."

Ellen gave him an appraising look. "I'll be interested to see what you come up with."

I said, "It's not really just Poppa, Ellen. They want lots of anecdotes about his famous clients, and that sort of thing."

Don laughed. "You may have to censor some of those. You know Poppa, Jane. He'll tell all! By the way, you two, how was the recital last night?"

I turned to Andrew. "What did you think? We haven't talked about it yet."

Andrew hesitated for a moment. "I should say that Gebler's technique is formidable and he has a good manner with the audience. As for Miss Bergstrom—well, I can say only that she's a true musician, very talented. They should both have fine careers before them. O'Connor Enterprises should do well for both of them."

Don said, "Actually, only Gebler is our client. I haven't met Miss Bergstrom, but I gather she declined an offer from us. She went with another agent."

At that moment Karl and Julie appeared and Don strode forward to shake hands with Karl Gebler. "I'm hearing great things from Dr. Quentin about last night."

Karl nodded, his dark face intense. "I think it went well. Yes, very well." Then he added casually, "Oh, Julie, this is Mr. Hubbard. He's the one who signed me up with O'Connor Enterprises after the competition."

I noticed with amusement Don's face as he shook hands with Julie. He had the look of a man who has just been handed an object of rare beauty but one so fragile he's afraid he might drop it.

A mild stir in the center of the lobby caught our attention, and Ellen remarked dryly, "Here comes her majesty."

And there indeed was Rosanna Rossi surrounded by a gaggle of news people and photographers. Her handsome young protégé stood to one side, looking on.

"It's miraculous," Ellen remarked. "She must be over fifty if she's a day, but who would believe it!"

Rosanna was indeed dazzling. She wore an immense picture hat of straw the color of a watermelon, under which her black hair was pulled back from her face and coiled at the back of her head. The creamy skin of her face and neck were remarkably smooth and firm, due, according to Ellen, to a sensational face-lift. Her dress of black silk minimized the plumpness of her body and a wisp of watermelon scarf added a dash to the ensemble. Her gorgeous black eyes flashed as she posed for the cameras and answered questions.

"Yes, for a whole week. It will be divine—resting and floating along through your beautiful French countryside. Ah, here is Monsieur O'Connor. Poppa, come, darling." She stretched an imperious hand and Poppa came to her side, his round face wreathed in smiles under the crown of white hair as the cameras flashed.

A moment later Rosanna announced, "That is all, ladies and gentlemen." Then suddenly she stopped. "No, wait, wait! This is Tonio Riccardi—the tenor. A divine voice. We will be rehearsing together for *La Bohème*."

The cameras flashed again. "Where will the performance be, Madame Rossi?"

"Ah, we cannot say yet." She smiled archly. "That is up to Mr. O'Connor. And now, thank you, ladies and gentlemen."

Then Molly presented to the group a young man who stood at her side.

"And now, everyone, this is Stephen Shaw, who will be our guide for the week."

I saw a blond Adonis clad in extremely tight pants and a safari jacket, his shirt unbuttoned halfway to his navel, a gold chain gleaming through the fair hair on his chest.

"Good morning, ladies and gentlemen." The accent

was British, the manner rather prim despite the sexy appearance. "It is indeed a pleasure for me to accompany such a distinguished group of guests"—with a gallant little bow in the direction of Rosanna—"aboard the *Jacqueline*. Since this is a private charter, we are, of course, entirely at your disposal. Mrs. O'Connor has suggested that we follow our usual itinerary from Dijon to Lyons, and we shall have our minibus available for those guests who wish to make the brief land tours which are normally provided. You will each find a schedule in your cabins when we reach the boat. If you are ready, then?"

We all clambered into a minibus and were in due course deposited at the Gare de Lyon, where Stephen Shaw piloted us to our seats on the high-speed train known as the T.G.V.

Once the train left the city, Andrew and I agreed that the French countryside we were passing through was incomparable. I had always found it hard to believe that those ancient red-roofed villages, each with its dominating church spire, tucked away among the green and wooded hills, were inhabited by real people and were not merely the inventions of an artist with an eye for the picturesque. The realities of French provincial life, as described by Balzac or Flaubert, were blurred by this distant view, like a Hollywood movie set seen in soft focus.

Our lunch was served on the train airplane-style, on a tray table in front of each seat.

"Oh, where are the snows of yesteryear?" moaned Andrew.

I knew what he meant. The elegant old dining cars of the past were an endangered species. "Be thankful there's food," I laughed. "My father and I once left Venice at six in the morning—too early for breakfast at the hotel—and had no food or drink till well into the afternoon. We learned then to travel with a Care package!''

As the train passed into the region of Burgundy, we began to have glimpses of medieval towns with their black slate roofs and ancient stone churches. Soon we would come into the region of the great vineyards, where some of the world's most exalted wines were produced.

I said, "I hear we're going to have fabulous food and wines on the cruise. And we're scheduled to visit some famous vineyards."

Andrew smiled. "I'm certainly glad we contracted to do the book on Poppa. It's going to be a marvelous week!"

6

At Dijon we were met by a minibus which took us to the banks of the River Saône, where we had our first glimpse of the charming barge that would be our hotel for the coming week. Above her black hull, the cabin gleamed in bright blue trimmed in red and adorned with painted flowers. White wrought iron tables and chairs dotted the forward deck, above the blunt prow where the name Jacqueline appeared on either side.

When we had all maneuvered the narrow metal gangplank with its hand ropes, and stepped into the main deck cabin, I noted with pleasure the luxurious appointments. A lounge area, with curved sofas of red plush on either side, looked inviting for conversation or for curling up with a good book. Polished wood gleamed everywhere, from the well-stocked bar with its shelves of bottles and glasses, to the walls and ceiling of the main salon. Tables of softly burnished wood, adorned with fresh flowers, stood on either side of the salon, where windows ran from ceiling to table level, keeping the outdoors always in view.

Now Stephen Shaw presented to us two tall young Frenchmen wearing blue jeans and pullovers, who stood in the dining area of the salon. "This is Emile, our captain, and Philippe, our chef. I have just learned that our stewardess is ill but she will no doubt be with us by the time dinner is served."

He cautioned us to keep our cabin windows closed whenever the boat was in motion, or we might find the cabin drenched with water. After he read out our cabin numbers, we trailed after him down carpeted stairs, past gleaming handrails and walls paneled in handsome wood, to find that our luggage had already been placed in our rooms.

Of the eight cabins on the lower deck, we learned that the two at either end were double in size, extending across the width of the boat. Poppa and Molly O'Connor shared the one at our left, and Rosanna, as most honored guest, was assigned to the other. The small cabin at the left of the stairs was assigned to Don, while Karl Gebler was given a cabin at the right of the stairs, and beyond him was Andrew, at the end next to Rosanna.

Opposite Andrew, and next to Rosanna on that end, was Tonio, with Julie in the center, and Ellen and I opposite Don and at the other end, next to Molly and Poppa.

At first glance Ellen and I thought our cabin was too tiny to hold both of us, but we soon found that the limited space was ingeniously arranged. There was a small but adequate closet, a washbasin with a cabinet below and a shelf above, all in the rich paneling that had prevailed above. Each bed had drawers beneath and shelves above, and a door led to a miniature bath with toilet and shower.

When we had stashed our things and started for the stairs, we heard Molly's voice calling, "Ellen, is that you, dear?"

Molly was standing in the doorway of the cabin next to ours, smiling at us. "Hello, girls."

Ellen and I exchanged a fleeting grin. We might be twenty-eight years of age to the rest of the world, but to Molly we would always be "the girls."

"Come and see our lovely cabin. I'm just getting Poppa settled for his rest."

Poppa was already tucked up in bed—was I destined to see him always in his pajamas?—and gave us the cherubic smile of the naughty child who is now on his best behavior.

Molly beamed. "Jane, I want you to see what Ellen brought us from Italy." Opening a travel case, Molly took out a stunning ruby glass decanter and two matching wineglasses, setting them out on the bedside table beside Poppa.

"They're lovely," I said.

Molly poured from an already opened bottle of wine into both glasses, taking a few sips from one. "Mmm, good." Opening a bottle of medicine, she handed Poppa two tablets and his wineglass.

Dutifully he took the tablets and drank off the glass in rapid gulps. "I like taking the pills with the wine," he said to me. "I can't taste them that way."

Molly asked, "How do you like the wine, dear?"

Poppa snorted. "You know I can't tell one wine from another. I like 'em all." He was clearly proud of his lack of discrimination—the diamond in the rough.

I said, "You know, Poppa, I hear we're going to have wonderful wines this week. Burgundy has some of the greatest vineyards in the world. Maybe you'll turn into an expert."

"Ho! That'll be the day."

As Ellen and I turned to go, Molly said, "I'll be up soon."

When we reached the foot of the stairs for the second time, we heard Rosanna's voice at the other end of the passage and saw Tonio Riccardi, the handsome tenor, standing in the doorway of Rosanna's wide cabin.

"Of course," murmured Ellen with a grin, "her ladyship has the other royal suite. I suspect Tonio won't spend much time in his own little lair."

"Wait for me, darling," Rosanna was saying, "I'll be ready in a minute."

From the cabin next to the stairs, a violin broke the silence with the beginning of practice scales, but as we reached the main deck the scales stopped abruptly and we heard Molly's voice—"Oh, Mr. Gebler, Mr. O'Connor is resting!"—and Karl Gebler's instant apology.

In the salon above we found Stephen Shaw, the guide, standing in the bar, idly arranging glasses and admiring his own reflection in the mirror. Seeing us, he turned and gave us a tight professional smile. "Do you care for something to drink?"

Ellen said, "It's only three o'clock. Too early for me, thank you," and I agreed. Looking at the etched glass of the bar, I said to Stephen, "It's rather like a London pub, isn't it?"

"Yes, it is, rather. Do you go to England often, Dr. Winfield?"

I noted that on the train to Dijon he had adroitly learned the names of the guests.

"I live in London. My husband is English."

"I see." He smiled, a shade more warmly this time.

Ellen looked into the dining area of the salon, then gestured to the grand piano standing against the wall on the left. "Do you usually have a piano aboard?"

"Oh, no, Mrs. Walker. Mr. O'Connor ordered it for the week. We took out two tables to fit it in. I understand some of the guests need it for rehearsal."

I remembered that Karl Gebler and Julie Bergstrom were scheduled for a recital at Lyon on Wednesday evening. Even if they repeated the Paris program, they would need rehearsal time. And, of course, Rosanna had told the newspeople that she and Tonio were rehearsing for *La Bohème*. I looked at the piano and thanked whatever gods there be that despite all my years of piano study, I had never been tempted to try for a concert career. For the performer, even on vacation, those hours of daily practice could seldom be skipped.

I saw Emile, the captain, take up the gangplank, coil the mooring rope, and sprint back to his post at the wheel, behind the superstructure on the main deck. Then the boat began to move.

Out on the deck we found Andrew and Don and were soon joined by Julie Bergstrom. Rosanna and Tonio emerged at the top of the stairs, but merely waved to us and headed for the bar. Only Karl Gebler and Molly—and, of course, Poppa—were still below.

Don said, "I wonder what's keeping Momma."

Ellen rolled her eyes. "Still fussing over Poppa, no doubt. She's given him his medicine. Maybe she's holding his hand till he goes to sleep."

When Karl did come above, he sat rather aloofly to one side, staring at the passing scene, while Molly, who had emerged after a quarter of an hour, looked uncharacteristically solemn, a slight frown on her usually cheerful countenance. Later on, when we learned what was worrying her, it seemed a minor problem. No one then could foresee the trouble that lay ahead.

7

The afternoon passed pleasantly, as the boat moved, smooth as glass, along the river, leaving the town of Dijon behind and in due course entering the Canal du Bourgogne, where the canal was often so narrow that you could almost reach out and touch the grassy banks. Sometimes fields of deepest green stretched away on either side, and sometimes rows of poplars clung so close that you felt you were passing slowly through an enchanted tunnel in a child's fairy story.

When we came to a lock in the canal, we saw the first of the quaint stone houses where the lockkeepers and their families lived. At each lock, children gave us friendly waves as the water slowly shifted to the proper level so that we could go on to the next segment of the canal.

The sun couldn't quite make up its mind whether to come out or hide behind the clouds, and when a cool breeze came up, I went down for a warmer sweater. As I came up into the salon, I saw Stephen Shaw setting out plates on the dining tables and gave him a friendly smile.

"This isn't my usual task, my dear. Isn't it dreadful? I shall have to serve the dinner as well!"

I sauntered over. "What happened?"

"The girl Francine was really very ill, poor thing. That's why we were a bit late leaving Dijon. Emile— the captain—took her to the hospital. It seems it's her appendix and they must operate. We've rung up the Paris office of Euro-Cruises, and meanwhile Emile says he's meeting someone at Longecourt who may be able to fill in for us."

"That would be helpful."

"Yes, indeed. He met the girl only this afternoon, before our party arrived in Dijon. She's on holiday from Paris and had come down to look at the boat, as she had been a temporary with Euro-Cruises last summer. It didn't take Emile long to make a date with her for this evening. He intends to persuade her to help us out this week, and I've no doubt he'll succeed. Young women are simply putty in his hands, my dear. He has only to flick his little finger."

And that's how sexy little Marie came to be aboard the *Jacqueline* that week.

Meanwhile, we had all drifted down to dress for dinner. By six o'clock everyone but Poppa and Molly had come up on deck and we had all helped ourselves to drinks at the bar. The pale June sun, high in the sky, still slipped in and out of the scudding clouds.

Tonio looked devastating in a dark blazer with an ascot tie, while Rosanna appeared in a flowered silk creation with a plunging neckline, a huge diamond pendant flashing on the magnificent bosom. The pair had begun a game of gin rummy on the observation deck, but Rosanna soon began to shiver.

"Let's go inside," she said, sweeping into the salon while Tonio was left to gather up cards, scorepad, and pencil.

Then Molly and Poppa appeared at the entrance to the salon. Poppa's dark suit was exquisitely tailored to make the most of his short, plump body, and Molly looked lovely in a simple dress of beige silk which brought out the brown of her eyes and hair. Everyone turned toward them and broke into a little spontaneous spatter of applause.

Poppa glowed in response. "Welcome, everyone. I hope you'll all have a great time this week." He moved among his family and guests, radiating the natural magnetism that people had for years found irresistible. Everyone seemed more alert when Poppa arrived. Rosanna, who had not bothered to exert herself before, began to sparkle. Tonio threw back his handsome head and laughed at some remark of Poppa's. Karl Gebler's intense face lighted in admiration, and Don looked on with his usual good-natured smile.

I thought at first that only Ellen, who had casually turned to look over a shelf of books, was immune to Poppa's charm. Then I caught sight of Julie Bergstrom, where she seemed to have shrunk into a corner behind the piano. Her beautiful eyes rested on Poppa in a kind of fixed stare. What could be wrong? I saw Don move toward her, standing protectively between her and Poppa's line of vision, as if he did not want Poppa to look over and see that hostile expression on Julie's face.

"Hello," I heard Don say to her rather inanely, and Julie looked at him with a start, her expression changing to one of relief. "Oh, hello," she said, mustering a pale smile.

Promptly at seven Molly moved toward the dining area, where two tables had been set, one for four and one for six. Molly and Poppa sat at the table for four and were joined by Rosanna and Tonio, the rest of us finding places at the other table.

Stephen Shaw, having apologized for the absence of the stewardess, then described the first wine to be served—a Pouilly-Fuissé from the Macon region, only a few miles from where we sat. When the wine had been poured, he brought the first course—a salmon mousse of such delicacy that *mmmms* and *ahhhs* arose spontaneously from both tables.

With each succeeding course and its accompanying wine, we soon saw that the promise of gourmet fare on the cruise was no idle boast, and Stephen, for all his moaning to me earlier about having to serve the food, managed the whole affair as if to service born.

Shortly after dinner we arrived at Longecourt, where some of us decided to leave the boat and go for a stroll. I noted with amusement that Don attached himself to Julie and Karl, while Andrew and Ellen and I formed a natural threesome. After a brief wander through the quiet streets of the little town, we stopped at a café across the street from the spot where the boat was moored.

At a nearby table sat Emile, our captain, with a girl who looked about nineteen or twenty. Slim, brown eyes, acquiline nose, brown hair pulled back in a ponytail, she looked like half the girls you saw in France, yet something in this girl made you look again. Emile's long legs were stretched under the table, a cigarette held negligently in his hand.

"So, Marie, what do you think?" he was saying.

Marie shrugged. "I'm not sure. How do you know the company will approve?"

"We've already asked. I'm to call them back."

I had no trouble following their rather idiomatic

French, since I had had the good fortune to spend a year in France as an exchange student at the age of sixteen, living with a family in a Paris suburb and attending school with my French "sister." My teenage slang might be out of date after twelve years, but my comprehension of French conversation was unimpaired.

I saw Emile and Marie look at each other, their eyes meeting in a long look. Then the girl shrugged again. Evidently this one was not as puttylike as Stephen had predicted.

Now the corners of her mouth turned up in a little half smile. "I can use the extra money."

Emile reached into his pocket and came up with a rather grubby envelope. "Here, write down your name and address and the dates you worked for the company last summer."

Marie took the pen he offered and wrote. Casually Emile took the envelope and strolled to the telephone on a back wall, where he dropped in some coins, returning in a few minutes.

"It's all arranged." Their eyes met again and this time they both smiled.

"Let's go," he said.

A few minutes later, as we left the café and paused on the bank to look down at the lighted salon of the *Jacqueline,* I saw Emile and Marie standing under the drooping branches of a tree, wrapped in a passionate embrace, his hand massaging the small of her back, her arms around him, one hand caressing the back of his neck. Stephen was right after all, I thought: Emile the Invincible.

Back on the boat, Don said an early good-night. "Still jet-lagging," he grinned. By half past ten Molly had settled Poppa for the night and come back above, where she had asked that Ellen and I wait for her.

"I'm so worried, girls," she began, having settled us in a corner of the salon. "I talked to Poppa about something this afternoon, but you know how he is—so stubborn if anyone suggests anything. Then I tried again just now, as he was going to bed, and he won't budge."

Ellen put her hand on her mother's arm. "But what is it, Momma?"

Molly's brown eyes half filled with tears. "It's about Poppa making a will. You see, dear, since we found out that Odette had a child by him, it will make all the difference in what happens to his estate. You and Don were never legally adopted, so you have no claim."

"Oh, Lord." Ellen looked stricken. "I never thought of that."

"It's so unfair to you children."

"Oh, it's not for myself that I care, Momma. It's for Don. Poppa has never even made him or Harry a partner in the business. I have a career that I love, and I wouldn't want to make a fuss about getting anything from Poppa anyway. But Don went into O'Connor Enterprises right out of college, and for almost nine years it's been his only professional life. If Poppa has an heir, he could inherit the bulk of the estate, including the business, and Don could be out in the cold."

Since Molly had asked me to stay, I thought I might as well get into the act. "Won't Poppa leave—well—quite a lot to you, Molly?"

"Oh, yes, that's just what he said. As matters were before, everything would go to me because Poppa has no living relations. But now it's quite a different story. What if I should go first? Then the French son would inherit it all! Of course, Poppa said that's unlikely, because he's seventy and I'm only fifty-five, but you never know what might happen.''

Ellen looked startled. "Momma, you *are* okay, aren't you? I mean, Dr. McLaren did say there's no sign of cancer?"

"Oh, yes, darling, of course. It isn't that. But accidents can happen to anybody. Or I could drop dead of a heart attack. If Poppa makes a will, I wouldn't have to worry."

"But he would want to provide for his own son too?"

"Oh, certainly." Molly smiled. "Remember, dear, your own father was a lawyer, and I still remember quite a lot about the law! What I suggested was that Poppa leave a life estate to me and the remainder in three equal shares, for his own son and for you and Don."

"That seems fair enough. Why won't he do it?"

"He has a thing about wills. I was afraid of that when I brought up the subject. The minute I said *will,* he just glared at me and said, 'I won't make a will and that's that. You know how I feel about it. My dad made a will and one month later he was dead. Thirty-six years old.' I pointed out that his father was already ill with tuberculosis when he made the will and that he did it to protect Poppa and his brother, but he just said, 'I don't care what you say. I won't do it.' "

I thought for a moment, then smiled. "I'm married to an English lawyer, Molly, and I'm learning a lot too. Don't you and Poppa hold most of your property in joint tenancy?"

"No, just our home and a few other pieces of property. Most of the big pieces of real estate are in his name only. He said they were business deals and he just didn't bother to put my name on them. I never made any objection before because it didn't seem to matter.''

''Yes, I see.''

''Of course, I'll talk to Don about it first thing in the morning, and he'll just say what you did, Ellen. Never mind about the money. But it matters to me. I'm not going to give up yet!''

8

Monday morning started out cool and cloudy. Our new stewardess, Marie, presided over the breakfast buffet with smiles and flips of her ponytail, apologizing for her English being "not too good."

As Poppa and I were the last to linger over our coffee, Marie looked down at the skirt she was wearing which she had pinned over at the waist and said to us with a giggle, "I don't have a skirt with me, so I must use this one of the other stewardess. The captain say I may go into the town quickly and buy one!"

"You'll look good in anything, Marie," said Poppa.

"Oh, thank you, Monsieur!"

Her mouth turned up in a little half smile which Poppa, and probably all other males in existence, would find bewitching.

"More coffee, Monsieur?"

"Yes, please, but it'll have to be the decaf. I have a bad heart, you know. Old age."

"But you are not old!"

Poppa beamed, and I left the two of them bantering

and set off across the gangplank and into the town in search of a battery for my camera. Never an ardent scene-snapper, I had taken one look at the weekly program and decided this was the time to exert myself and return to James with a collection of slides for the projector.

Needless to say, no sooner had everyone moaned about the weather than the sun broke through and firmly demonstrated that it knew all along it was summer. Having found a shop and dealt with the camera, I peeled off my sweater, checked my watch, and found that there was time for a quick walk. I followed the twisting street up the hill until the last of the houses gave way to open fields and woods. A narrow but paved road wound away through the trees on my right. From here I could look down over the village to the tree-lined canal where the *Jacqueline* lay in the water, looking for all the world like a child's brightly colored toy.

Suddenly I heard the sound of a motorcycle starting up. Looking along the road to where it bent out of sight under the trees, I saw Marie standing beside a figure on a Honda. The rider's back was toward me but I saw a slender body dressed in black pants, a turtleneck, and a black stocking cap, and caught a glimpse of a small black mustache as the man turned to speak to Marie.

The two were talking earnestly, their whole demeanor one of familiarity. This was not a stranger asking directions, I thought. It's someone she knows. I watched for a few moments more as Marie listened and nodded her head, apparently in agreement. Then I turned and walked quickly down the hill, not wanting the girl to see me observing her.

At the bottom of the hill I saw Emile sitting at an

outdoor table of a little café and paused to say, "Lovely day, isn't it?"

"Oui, madame." He spoke civilly but with none of the social graces of Stephen, our English guide.

Idly, I asked, "Do you enjoy running the boat?"

He gave me a sardonic smile. "I grew up in Marseille, where my uncle taught me everything about ships—real ships. Now they call me captain—of *that!*" He gestured toward the *Jacqueline*.

As there seemed to be no suitable reply to this, I merely waved and walked on. Then behind me I heard Marie's voice and turned to see her come swinging down the hill, looking innocently cheerful.

I heard Emile ask, "Did you find a skirt?"

"No, no luck." Marie's voice floated after me as I approached the boat.

I smiled to myself, thinking Emile may have met his match after all.

By eleven o'clock Andrew and I were settled with Poppa under the umbrella of a table on the deck to begin our first interview for the biography. We had agreed that Andrew would operate his tape recorder while we both took notes of anything that crossed our minds as we went along. As the boat moved along the canal, I thought of the sizable advance we had been given for the book on Poppa, and smiled. It was hard to believe that floating through this enchanted world of trees and country vistas could really be work for which we were being paid.

"Okay," said Poppa, "fire away."

Andrew smiled. "We may as well begin at the beginning. Why don't you tell us something about your early life?" He switched on the tape and Poppa began describing his childhood in Brooklyn with parents who were both immigrants from Ireland.

"My grandparents were Protestant Irish from the north, so my brother and I went to public instead of parochial school. My dad worked in a printer's shop. In those days they really picked up each piece of type and dropped it into a slot. I remember being allowed to watch and wondering how they could work so fast. When I was twelve my mother died. My kid brother was only eight, and I had to look after him till dad got home. Then four years later our father died. I was sixteen and I quit school and went to work to support my brother. That's when I got the name Poppa. My little brother began calling me that—just to kid me. But the name stuck and everybody's called me that ever since."

As Poppa recounted incidents from his youthful days we could hear Rosanna's voice doing the scales and roulades of the singer's daily practice. Presently Tonio's tenor floated up, their vocalizing forming a musical background to Poppa's reminiscences.

After a time Poppa reached the period when his professional life began.

"I got into the agency racket sort of by accident. See, I had a couple of pals who did song-and-dance numbers, and one of 'em starting hitting the big time. He brought the other guy up with him and they both had me start doing bookings for them. They were lousy businessmen, and when I worked deals and got good contracts for them I started charging a small fee. At first it was less than the percentages of the regular agents, so some of their friends started using me too. Then Eddie Kelly—nobody remembers him now, but he was pretty popular in those days—well, Eddie married a gal who was an opera singer and through her I got a lot of clients in longhair music."

"Then you have no musical training or background?"

Poppa gave an impish grin. "Nope. I was strictly on the business side of things. I managed their money for 'em when they wanted me to and doled out allowances to some who couldn't keep two nickels together without somebody being a watchdog. So pretty soon I raised my fees and found I could make a good living that way. In the depression years you would think there wouldn't be any business, but I always kept going. Then after the war things really began to boom."

"How did you happen to come to California?"

"Well, my brother had been killed in the war, so I had no family in New York. Then by the 1950s I found that I was going out to the coast a lot and I finally decided to open an office out there and leave Harry in New York. That's Harry Cocklin. He's been my right-hand man for years. Another thing was—well, my first wife left me around that time. See, I was married to this French gal—what a spitfire she was. A real crazy woman. After two years of pure hell she took off. Right at Christmastime too. I guess I was relieved, but I was also pretty upset. Anyway, it seemed like a good time for a change of scene."

Poppa looked up as Karl Gebler appeared on the deck.

"Excuse me, Mr. O'Connor. Will it disturb you if we rehearse?"

Poppa waved a genial hand. "No, go ahead. That's why I got the piano for you." Then, to Andrew, "He's a great young guy, isn't he?"

We saw Julie walk into the salon with her music and presently we heard the sounds of the Ravel sonata for violin and piano which the young pair had done at the recital in Paris.

Meanwhile, the rest of the party had come above. Ellen and Don, taking advantage of the weather, donned swim suits and were stretched out on mats on the far side of the deck, with Molly in a chair nearby. In the salon Rosanna and Tonio had resumed their gin rummy game, and their cries of protest or triumph punctuated the music of Karl and Julie's rehearsal.

"So when I had been in Los Angeles for a while," Poppa went on, "that was when I met Molly. She had been an actress before she married Hubbard. He had died the year before and she had these two little kids. She had some bit parts in films but it was tough sledding for her. She was a real beauty in those days."

"She still is," said Andrew, smiling.

Poppa looked slightly startled. "Oh, yeah, she is, isn't she? Well, I'll say this. The day I married Molly was my lucky day. What a difference from that bitch Odette!"

For some time Poppa continued the story of the years spent developing his agency, describing the growth of the staff, the decision in the sixties to make Los Angeles the home office, the need for constant travel on the part of his agents when important artists needed personal attention, the ways he had developed of coping with the temperamental ones—"which is most of them," he grinned.

Suddenly Poppa paused and looked at us. "Listen, you two. You seem like a really nice guy, Andrew, and I've known Jane here since she was a kid. Why don't you turn off that tape for a minute? I've got a problem, and I'd like to know what you think about it."

"Of course." I knew Andrew was surprised. I had told him Poppa was uninhibited, but Andrew was himself so reticent that I knew he found it hard to believe that people like Poppa were willing, even eager, to discuss their personal lives with anyone who would listen. That the problem was personal was clear enough from Poppa's request to stop the tape.

Just as Poppa began to speak, Emile and Marie came on to the forward deck.

"Excuse me, sir," Emile said to Poppa. "We are coming to a lock in the canal and I wish to show Marie about the ropes." He gave the girl some instructions and slipped back to the stern.

Poppa shrugged and turned to Andrew. "Jane already knows about this. See, here's what happened." And he plunged into the story of his phone call from his former wife, Odette, and the fact that he was the father of a son now in his twenties. He had raised his voice in order to be heard over the sound of the music, and suddenly, just as Karl and Julie stopped playing for a moment, Poppa's voice rang out for everyone to hear: "And now that I've found out I have a kid of my own, she wants me to make a will!"

9

There was a moment of frozen silence on the *Jacqueline* when Poppa's voice rang out. Across the deck Molly's arm stopped midway as she was in the act of pointing out to Don and Ellen something in the passing scene. Marie, standing at the rail, turned her head sharply and stared at Poppa in surprise. In the salon Tonio paused as he was reaching toward the pack to draw a card, looking at Rosanna with a startled expression. Karl Gebler stood with his bow in midair, looking out toward Poppa. Julie sat at the piano, her head down, her hands lying motionless on the keys. Then quickly she broke the awkward silence with a series of random chords on the piano. Voices began to murmur and the spell was broken.

I could see that poor Andrew was acutely embarrassed until he realized that Poppa was serenely oblivious to the whole incident. Leaning toward us as if nothing had happened, Poppa went on with his story.

"See, the reason I don't want to make a will is, my father did and a month later he was dead. Call it superstition—and sure, he already had TB—but I always thought he might have gotten well if he hadn't done that. It's like—well, you know—like saying 'I give up. Come and get me.' See what I mean? So what do you think?''

I knew perfectly well that like most people who ask for advice, Poppa merely wanted his own opinion confirmed, but I thought I might as well get in my two cents worth.

"Don't you want to provide for your new son, Poppa?" I asked innocently.

"Oh, sure, but I can do that while I'm still around, can't I? I'll be meeting him next week. I'll find out what kinda guy he is.''

"Then what about—er—Don and Ellen?"

"Oh, Molly will take care of them when I'm gone."

I felt that I had better not press further, and Poppa said, "Well, Andrew, what do you think?"

Andrew adroitly avoided committing himself on the subject, and soon steered Poppa back to the tape recording.

A few minutes later, when Andrew stopped to turn the tape cassette to the other side, all was quiet again as Karl and Julie had stopped to change their music scores. As Andrew switched on the tape, he accidentally pressed the play button and a soprano voice soared into the silence, singing the beginning of the "Liebestod" from Wagner's *Tristan and Isolde*. Rosanna stepped out onto the deck and signaled to Andrew that she was listening.

"Is that Flagstad?" she asked.

Andrew smiled. "That's right! I taped this for a class at the university one day and had forgotten it was on the cassette."

"That was some voice," said Rosanna. "I used to hear Traubel at the Met when I was a kid in New York, but I've heard Flagstad only on recordings. Of course, I've never sung Wagner myself, but I've always admired those tremendous gals like Flagstad and Traubel and Nilsson.''

"Which was the best, do you think?"

"Oh, they were all great, but I think Flagstad had a purity of tone that can't be beat."

Rosanna strolled back into the salon, and we went on with our interview until about twelve-thirty, when Poppa suggested we quit for the day.

"You make this really easy." He clapped Andrew on the back. "I didn't know what to expect—you being a professor from a big university and all that."

As we walked away from the table, Poppa stumbled slightly against a protrusion on the deck.

"What the hell is that thing?" Poppa looked down at a cube about three feet square which seemed to be fastened to the deck. Don walked over and studied the object. Bending over, he tried to lift it and found that one side came up while the other was hinged to the deck. Inside were some wooden rungs leading down into darkness.

"Of course, it's a hatch," Don said. "Down below there is a wooden ladder against the wall next to my cabin. I guess it's for emergency, and this is where it comes out."

Andrew said, "I think I'll stick to the stairs," and, laughing, we all went below to get ready for lunch.

Throughout the morning the boat had passed through several locks in the canal and now had moored near a village that looked as if it might have survived intact from the Middle Ages, with its ancient stone buildings and the spire of its church rising grandly upward.

When the party took their places for lunch—which

turned out to be another divine meal—I noticed that Rosanna and Tonio sat again with Poppa and Molly.

Andrew murmured to me, "It looks as if the six at our table are presumably the 'young' crowd, except for poor Tonio. He must be a good deal younger than I am, but he's stuck with the elders!"

I laughed. "I suspect Rosanna won't let him out of her sight."

After lunch the minibus arrived to take us on our first tour of the area.

"Poppa must have his afternoon rest," Molly explained, "but I'm glad everyone else can come along."

As Poppa started down the stairs, we heard Rosanna say, "You'll be on the phone to Harry this afternoon, won't you, Poppa? Remember, I want to know about Glyndebourne."

Molly was the last to join the group on the minibus.

"Sorry to keep you waiting," she said. "I've put Poppa's medicine by his bed and poured his wine. He can be careless and not take the right amount of tablets, which the doctor said is dangerous.

"Why don't you give them to him yourself," Momma?" Don asked.

"Oh, he wants to talk to Harry before he takes his nap."

As the minibus moved through the lush green of the countryside, I noted that Stephen Shaw, for all his rather fussy manner, was an excellent guide. He made brief but intelligent comments from time to time without smothering us with more facts than anyone would reasonably want to know.

Our first stop, at the abbey at Citeaux, proved to be a stirring experience. Stephen led us silently into a barren stone chapel, where we took seats on plain wooden benches. Presently the monks began to enter from the back of the chapel, one by one, each one moving down the central aisle and taking his place on benches facing those where the visitors sat. When the last one had found his place, there was a further moment of silence. Then the voices of the monks began to sing the Gregorian chants that had remained unchanged for centuries. I found myself curiously moved by the modal music, with its purity and its reminder of an era before the diatonic scale came into use. When the music ended and the last of the monks had left the chapel, the visitors rose and filed out in silence, each one unwilling to break the spell.

Outside in the sunshine I stood with Andrew and Ellen.

"Lovely, wasn't it?" she said, her green eyes glowing, "but it does make one wonder about the life of the ascetic. What are the impulses that cause some individuals to give up the pleasures of the world?"

Andrew looked at her thoughtfully. "For myself I would find it utterly impossible. I am not much of a hedonist, but I think I would find life intolerable without some varieties of experience."

Ellen nodded. "Yes, exactly. Even more than the obvious sensual pleasures, one would miss the aesthetic ones—all the music of the last three centuries, all the painting, the architecture, and so on."

"And the pleasures of travel," Andrew added, smiling at her. I had noticed at dinner the evening before that they had discovered a shared passion for Italy.

"So, then," Ellen pursued, "what is the function of the ascetic? I suppose it stands as a symbol of virtue for those who indulge in worldly excess. For people who have acquired power, for example, it may even represent the principle of justice."

I wondered if she was thinking of Poppa. Her stepfather had acquired power and was using it unfairly against her beloved brother. A young woman with Ellen's independent spirit might be more deeply stirred by this injustice than any of us would imagine.

Back in the minibus, we drove along through the region of the Côte d'Or, or "golden slope," where many of the finest red Burgundies were produced, with Stephen telling us something about the factors of soil and climate that produce the great wines. We stopped at a famous château to see the huge presses and other paraphernalia for the making of the wines and were given a quick course in the rituals of wine-tasting—warming the glass with the hand, sniffing the bouquet, swishing the wine over the tongue, inhaling through the nose, and so on.

Afterward, while we walked around the grounds before boarding the bus, Andrew and I saw Julie Bergstrom sitting alone on a bench under a tree, her head slightly bowed. When we sat down beside her she looked up with a brief hello and dropped her head again. Then, in an obvious attempt to make conversation, she said, "I don't think I'll ever be any good at wine-tasting. I'm not sure I even like red wine. I like only the white."

Andrew smiled. "You're probably too young," he said lightly. "At your age my tastes didn't go much beyond hamburgers and root beer."

Having established himself as the ancient mariner, Andrew evidently decided to pursue his fatherly role.

"Julie," he said quietly, "something is bothering you. Do you want to talk about it?"

The beautiful eyes looked at us, their blue deepened by the reflection of the sky.

"I suppose I may as well tell you." She sighed. "I've tried not to let it show, but I feel so depressed. I tried to get out of coming on this trip, but Karl wouldn't hear of it. You see, I really hate Mr. O'Connor!''

I said, ''But I didn't know you had met him before.''

''I hadn't, but I grew up hating the sound of his name.''

Once she had begun, Julie poured out the story in a rush. ''My brother was a wonderful violinist. He's much older and I sort of worshipped him as I was growing up. Well, twelve years ago Eric was winning competitions and seemed to be on his way to a big career. It meant everything to him. It was his whole life. He signed a contract with Mr. O'Connor and after a while everything just dried up. He had good notices when he did play, but what it came down to is that Mr. O'Connor just didn't like him. Eric is very serious and not good at buttering up people like Mr. O'Connor, I guess. Now Eric is teaching at a college in Iowa—''

Julie broke off, looking at Andrew with a flushed face. ''Oh, I'm sorry, I didn't mean to sound as if teaching is the end of the world.''

Andrew smiled. ''No, I understand perfectly. Teaching was not what your brother wanted. Jane and I know people at the university who are disappointed concert performers and they still carry the scars.''

''What makes me so furious,'' Julie went on, ''is to see someone like Karl getting all the attention—and the bookings—when Eric was so much better. Karl has great technique, but he doesn't have any real feeling for music.''

''Yes,'' Andrew said cautiously, ''that was my impression of Karl at the recital in Paris, but I didn't want to express an opinion. In fact, I thought perhaps he was your boyfriend—''

For the first time I saw Julie's face break out in a smile. ''Karl? Not in a million years. He's not interested, and neither am I. Anyhow, now you can see why I tried to get out of coming on the boat this week.''

''Did you tell Karl the reason?''

''Oh, yes, but he said that was ridiculous. It's pretty hard to dent that giant ego. Would you believe he was very upset because he got only the silver medal instead of the gold at the competition? Anyhow, the problem is, I had to admit he was right when he said there was no way I could explain why I wouldn't want to come on the cruise. I certainly don't want to lose my chance to work with Karl. I've had some professional appearances, but this is my first time to make fairly good money. So I had to come along. There was no way out.''

On the drive back to the *Jacqueline,* Julie seemed more relaxed than she had been earlier, chatting happily with Don and Ellen. Evidently, talking about her problem had eased her mind.

Andrew, sitting next to me, was silent for much of the short trip. Then he said rather diffidently, ''Your friend Ellen is quite a remarkable person. She reminds me a little of Norma.''

I looked at him in surprise, remembering his wife's merry dark eyes and fluff of brown hair.

''Oh, not in appearance.'' He smiled. ''Perhaps it's her straightforward way of looking and speaking. It's not really a resemblance—just a quality of some kind—''

All my matchmaking instincts were thoroughly aroused, but I merely said, ''Yes, Ellen's a very special person.''

I remembered James's flippant remark that I should find a wife for Andrew, and I thought how lovely it would be if these two dear friends should come to care for each other.

10

Back on the *Jacqueline* we were scattered about on the deck when we heard Rosanna say to Tonio, "Dar-ling, why don't you go and get the *Bohème* score? We have ages before dinner. We can go over some passages together."

Tonio set off down the stairs and Rosanna turned to Julie with an imperious gesture. "You'll play for us, won't you, dear?"

Don gave a start and looked at Julie, who stared at Rosanna but said nothing.

Don spoke first. "Rosanna, really! Julie—Miss Bergstrom—is an artist, not a rehearsal pianist."

Rosanna's eyebrows shot up and she looked from Don to Julie and back with an expression which clearly said "Oh-ho!" An expert in affairs of the heart, she took in Don's worshipful gaze and Julie's look of gratitude. Nevertheless, she wanted someone on the piano and her black eyes began to flash.

At this point Andrew and I more or less simultaneously offered our services. I said, "Look, I'll be glad to play for you," while Andrew was saying, "Let me—"

Rosanna turned to Andrew and studied him for a moment. Then she gave him the full force of her brilliant smile. "Thank you, er"—obviously groping for his name—"Andrew!" Her eyes held his and her expression quite plainly said, What an attractive man you are—I hadn't noticed before!

After a bit of Alphonse and Gaston-ing, I persuaded Andrew to stay where he was and I took my place at the piano as Tonio arrived with the score.

"Thank you, Jane!" I got the full blaze of Rosanna's dazzling smile as she indicated a scene in Act Three she wanted to work on and I soon began to enjoy the occasion. Even singing in half-voice for rehearsal, Rosanna and Tonio sounded marvelous, and as they worked through the great passage in which Rodolfo and Mimi cannot bear to part and agree to stay together until the spring, I learned to my surprise that Rosanna was what's known in the trade as an "intelligent" singer. Like the famed Maria Callas, Rosanna was not content merely to "sound beautiful"; she worked to give each phrase a dramatic color and meaning. Tonio listened and followed her directions with respect.

When they paused to rest, Rosanna began explaining to me her plan to do the opera with Tonio at Glyndebourne the following summer.

"You see, they have already asked for Tonio to sing Rodolfo and they have not yet cast Mimi, as I happen to know. I've asked Poppa to tell them I'm willing to take the part. I sang Elvira in *Don Giovanni* there when I was young and I've always intended to go back. Of course, it's not much money, but now I can afford to do as I like. Poppa claims that he has already asked for me and they said no, but that's ridiculous.

I'm at the peak of my career, and no opera house in the world would turn me down!''

Egotistical as Rosanna's statement sounded, it was probably pretty much true. Ironically, Glyndebourne was one of the few opera houses in the world that might turn her down. I knew that the renowned Glyndebourne Festival Theatre, nestled in the hills of Sussex, south of London, had established a reputation for both musical and dramatic fidelity to the text. Rehearsals were lengthy and meticulous, unlike those of most houses, and the singers were selected not for their big names but for their suitability to the role. Despite the astronomical prices of the tickets, the singers were paid far less than the fees a singer like Rosanna could command at huge houses like La Scala in Milan or the Metropolitan in New York.

Rosanna's problem was that at her age and with her weight it was extremely unlikely that Glyndebourne would want her in the role of the frail young seamstress who dies of consumption at the end of the opera. If she had wanted the prestige of singing at Glyndebourne again, I thought, she should have done it years before. How curious that she could be so thoroughly professional in her work and yet seemingly unable to see for herself that she was no longer right for singing Mimi at Glyndebourne.

After an hour or so of work, Rosanna thanked me quite graciously for my help and suggested we break for the day. "Poppa should have some news for me soon. He was planning to call his office this afternoon. Won't it be marvelous, darling"—to Tonio—"to work together?"

By dinnertime Monday everyone aboard the *Jacqueline* had heard about the crisis in the O'Connor family. Earlier that day, when Poppa's voice had rung out in the momentary silence with the words "Now that I've found out I have a kid of my own, she wants me to make a will," everyone who didn't already know the circumstances was avid to learn what it was all about. During the afternoon tour Rosanna had managed to get the whole story from Molly. Rosanna told Tonio, who in turn passed the information on to Karl and Julie.

Even the crew had their own somewhat incomplete version of the story, according to Stephen Shaw, who seemed to have adopted me as his confidante. When I came up for the cocktail hour, Stephen drew me aside. "One can't help hearing *everything* on a boat this size, Jane." We had arrived at first names by this time. "My dear, we were absolutely agog when Mr. O'Connor's voice soared out, saying he had just learned about a long-lost child. Marie overheard some conversation about a son by a former wife."

Stephen paused suggestively, but I merely murmured, "Mmm," a phrase I had learned from James which covered a multitude of omissions.

"Philippe had heard nothing," Stephen went on. "When he isn't cooking, he has his ears covered with his eternal headset, listening to rock music. But our captain was frightfully interested. He said, 'If Mr. O'Connor made a will, would it be to include his son or to leave him out?' and I said he would have to name him in the will but the amount he left to him could be a great deal or only a token. Isn't that correct?"

"Yes, I expect so," I said vaguely.

Needless to say, none of the speculations on the part of his guests and crew reached Poppa's ears. Blandly unaware of having caused a stir, Poppa came up to join his guests. The warm weather had held throughout the day, and we had all taken our drinks out to the observation deck.

Poppa and Rosanna were soon the center of an animated group exchanging anecdotes of performances.

"I do think singing Gilda is the worst," cried Rosanna. "That god-awful sack. I always think I'll suffocate."

Poppa chuckled. "Whenever Rosanna sings *Rigoletto* we write into her contract that the sack must have plenty of holes!"

"I'd never do it if it weren't for *'Cara nome,'* " laughed Rosanna. "That aria makes up for everything."

Tonio described an incident at a performance of *Tosca* in a small opera house in Italy. "In Act One Cavaradossi is supposed to be painting a portrait in the church when Tosca comes in. Unfortunately the prop man forgot to provide the paintbrush. There I am, holding the palette and studying the painting, but I cannot make a stroke!"

As Poppa stood beaming at the center of the smiling group, Rosanna casually asked, "Well, Poppa, what did you find out about Glyndebourne?"

Poppa's smile faded and he looked acutely uncomfortable.

"Look, Rosanna," he said, "we can talk about it later."

"Later?" Rosanna's black eyes kindled. "What do you mean, later? We'll talk about it now."

Poppa sighed. "Okay. I talked to Harry and he says Glyndebourne is looking for a *young* soprano for Mimi. I hate to say it so bluntly, sweetie, but you see the problem. Instead of singing 'Mimi,' Rodolfo would have to sing 'Mama.' "

Poppa looked around as if seeking applause for his witticism but elicited only a weak smile from Karl Gebler and averted eyes from the rest of us.

Rosanna glared. "That's not funny, Poppa. Look, they really want Tonio, don't they? Well, all you have to do is tell them they can't have him unless they take me too. We're both under contract to you, and you can do that easily. You've done it before for people when you wanted to."

Oblivious to their embarrassed listeners, Poppa and Rosanna pursued their quarrel, their voices rising as their anger increased.

"Oh, hell, Rosanna, I'm too old to put up that kind of a fight. And besides, you don't want to stand in Tonio's way, do you?"

"I'm *not* standing in Tonio's way. I want him to have the part, of course. I simply want to do it with him. You just tell them I'm part of the package. They'll knuckle under."

Poppa's eyes turned to blue steel in anger. "I won't do it, Rosanna, so lay off, will you?"

Rosanna's face hardened, revealing unlovely lines. "Don't you give me that steely-eyed look, Poppa O'Connor. Everybody else may crawl on their hands and knees to you, but not *me*. I want that part, and you better do as I say or you'll be sorry."

She swept regally into the salon, followed by Tonio, where he could be seen preparing another cocktail for her and listening to her protests.

When dinner was announced, Rosanna ostentatiously took her seat at the table on the opposite side of the boat from the O'Connor table, with Tonio beside her. I saw Andrew and Don exchange slight smiles as with one accord they joined Poppa and Molly at their table, while the rest of us sat with Tonio and Rosanna. We could hear Poppa chatting away in the best of spirits, seemingly unaffected by his battle with Rosanna.

Dinner featured an exquisite *boeuf bourguignon,*

which drew murmurs of appreciation from both tables. Even Poppa, who prided himself on having no taste buds, acknowledged that the beef was "about the best I ever ate."

During the past few hours the boat had stopped to pass through several locks in the canal. Now it had stopped again, and as we were finishing the desert course—a divine *tarte citron*—the captain, Emile, stepped into the salon and beckoned to Stephen Shaw. They conferred for some time, and then Stephen asked the group for their attention.

"Ladies and gentlemen, we have encountered a slight problem. The lock ahead of us is the last one we pass through before reaching our destination for the night. Unfortunately, we have received word that there has been minor damage to the lock and we don't know how soon it can be repaired. Meanwhile we shall remain here. Please feel free to leave the boat and walk or bicycle on the towpaths alongside the canal. If the boat should move forward while you are on land, don't be alarmed. You may wish to watch while we pass through the lock and you can rejoin the boat on the other side."

Poppa looked up at Stephen. "What happens if they don't fix the lock?"

"Then we shall simply remain here for the night, sir. There should be no problem. Two barges behind us are similarly held up and will be waiting for the same reason."

Molly said, "Thank you, Stephen. I'm sure we'll be fine." Then to the rest of us, "Let's change into comfortable clothes and go exploring!"

11

Everyone seemed in good spirits as we gathered on the deck in our casual garb.

"Half past nine and still so light!" cried Rosanna.

Karl turned toward her with his slightly disdainful air. "It is only a few days until the summer solstice."

"Oh, yes, I suppose so." Rosanna looked vaguely at Karl, then took Tonio's arm. "Come, darling, let's go for a walk."

Ellen and I were looking over the bicycles with Don and Julie when Andrew came up, saying, "I haven't ridden a bike for years, but I'd like to try."

Behind us we heard Poppa's voice. "But, Doll, why don't I just sit here on the deck?"

Molly spoke firmly. "No, dear, you know you're supposed to walk every day. You wriggled out of it yesterday and so far today. So off you go. I'll come out as soon as I've finished my postcards."

Since Karl declined any interest in biking, the five of us steered our bikes down the narrow gangplank and began riding along the towpath toward the lock that had caused the delay. I looked back and saw Poppa come down to the towpath and set off in the opposite direction, where he was soon out of sight around a bend in the canal.

Andrew had no trouble renewing his bicycle skills. After one or two wobbles, he was skimming along with the rest of us. We stopped briefly at the lock, where the canal narrowed and passed between stone abutments, a little walking bridge spanning the water where the two arms of the closed lock came together. Assorted people from the surrounding area had gathered to watch the workmen as they bent over the mechanism. Nothing seemed to be happening, so we rode on in single file along the towpath, with Don and Ellen in the lead. I breathed in the balmy air, wishing James could be here. Poor angel, slaving away in London. Maybe we should consider coming back here to Burgundy for our August holiday.

Daydreaming about James, I hit a bump that spilled me over onto the towpath. By the time Andrew and Julie had disentangled me from my bicycle and I had determined that I was neither bloody nor bowed, we saw that Ellen and Don were out of sight around a curve in the canal. When we finally caught up with them, we found them sitting on a log in a little clearing, talking earnestly.

"Pull up a stump," Don said cheerily as we arranged ourselves in a rough circle. The light was fading quickly now, and in the half dark we felt a sense of intimacy.

Ellen said, "We were talking about Poppa and the will. It's no secret now, so we may as well ask your opinion. Don wants to go to Poppa and tell him he doesn't care about his making a will."

Don looked up. "I don't like the idea of Momma

urging Poppa to do something he doesn't want to do. I know he hates the thought of making a will."

Ellen went on. "But I've pointed out that O'Connor Enterprises has been Don's whole life ever since college, and if Poppa has a child of his own, the man could inherit not only the bulk of the estate but the business as well."

Don frowned. "I have to admit Ellie has a point there. Harry and I could run the business, take our salaries, have all the headaches, and then give the profits—and maybe the control—to some French guy we've never seen."

Andrew said, "What about simply asking Poppa to give you full partnership in the firm now?"

Ellen nodded. "I agree. That would help."

Don shook his head. "Actually, I've hinted at that more than once, but Poppa feels that that's in the same category as making a will. He says it's like giving up and saying he's on the shelf. He can be pretty pigheaded, I admit."

I said, "Not only that, Don, you'd hate to see the business go to someone else, I imagine."

"Yeah, I would. There are some changes I want to make when Poppa—er—retires. For one thing, we need to eliminate some of the favoritism that he goes in for."

I saw Julie's eyes light up as she looked at Don. Now, I thought, she can tell him about her brother. Until now she would have assumed that Don was part of the O'Connor establishment and not to be trusted.

We talked on for a few minutes but reached no useful conclusions and soon started riding back toward the lock, where we found the workers still hovering over their task. Looking back, I noticed that we had lost Don and Julie and I smiled to myself. Then I went back to the boat for a warmer jacket, and as I returned to the area of the lock, I heard a hoarse cry, followed by a splash, and knew that someone must have fallen into the canal.

I ran toward the grassy bank and looked down into the dark water, where I heard the sound of someone thrashing about. Pulling off my shoes and jacket, I was about to leap in, when I heard another splash. Seconds later a pair of strong arms had lifted the victim, and I could just make out a crown of white hair emerging from the water.

"Poppa!" I cried out.

Gasping and choking, Poppa was carried the few feet to the bank of the canal. Someone at the lock turned the floodlight under which they had been working so that the whole scene was illuminated like a movie set. Tonio appeared beside me, and together we reached for Poppa's arms and helped him out of the water and up onto the grass.

By this time people were converging from all directions. Don ran up and threw himself down beside his stepfather. Stephen Shaw took one look, and saying, "I'll get some blankets," ran toward the *Jacqueline*.

Sputtering with rage, Poppa sat up, glaring at the faces that crowded around him. "Somebody pushed me!" he shrieked.

Now we saw the dripping figure of a boy who looked about fourteen. "The gentleman is safe?" he asked in heavily accented English.

It proved to be the lockkeeper's son, who had plunged into the water at the first sound of the splash and scooped Poppa up so promptly.

"Yes," I said to the boy. "I'm sure he'll be fine. Thank you so very much!"

We had wrapped Poppa's shivering body in whatever jackets and sweaters came to hand, and as the boy turned to go, Poppa whimpered, "I'm not fine,

Jane. I'm freezing. And what's more, I never learned to swim. I could've been drowned!''

Now Stephen Shaw arrived, bringing blankets, with Molly beside him.

''Oh, Molly!'' Poppa stood up unsteadily and threw his arms around his wife. ''Somebody pushed me into the water, Doll. Somebody tried to kill me!''

It seems that when Poppa left the *Jacqueline* he turned away from the lock, as I had noticed, and walked back along the towpath, moving briskly, as his doctor had told him to do. Once started on his walk, Poppa had to admit that he enjoyed the exercise. The balmy air felt good, and it was still light enough to see where he was going—no danger of tripping on the path.

On his left, he told Molly, Poppa passed the two barges which were waiting behind the *Jacqueline* for the lock to be repaired. One carried cargo and the other appeared to be a houseboat with a family aboard. He heard a baby crying and the voice of the mother soothing the infant, and he thought about what he had missed by not knowing that he had a child of his own. Apparently he even shed a sentimental tear or two as he pictured himself holding an infant in his arms. Now he had missed twenty-five years of his son's life, but he would make it up somehow. If only that bitch Odette had told him where to find her. When Saturday came and they were back at the Meurice, she would surely call.

Lost in thought, Poppa had walked rapidly on. Suddenly he stopped. The light was no longer coming through the branches of the trees lining the canal. Darkness was falling quickly. Poppa turned and went back the way he had come, unable to move as rapidly as before for fear of stumbling over unseen hazards.

His eyes on the ground, he could hear sounds all around him where everything had seemed so silent before. The water lapped softly at his right; the trees over his head rustled; the low putt-putt of a motorcycle sounded somewhere nearby.

Twice in the next few minutes Poppa was sure he heard footsteps approaching on the path, and once he passed a dark figure going in the opposite direction. Rustling noises in the shrubbery to his left made him start. Then he heard footsteps behind him. His heart began to thud and his breath came faster. An unreasoning fear gripped him and he tried to run. Suddenly his foot caught in a rut in the path and he fell sprawling on the ground. His knee was bruised and his hands stung where he had tried to break his fall.

Panic-stricken, he got awkwardly to his feet and began to limp along the path, his breath coming in short gasps. He had always been afraid of the dark, and although he knew the fear to be ridiculous, he couldn't control the pounding of his heart. He no longer heard the footsteps behind him, but now and then there were crackling and rustling sounds that added to his terror.

On his right he caught a glimpse of the houseboat and another dark shape in the canal that must be the cargo barge. Then, as the canal made a turn, he saw the *Jacqueline*, but there was no sign of anyone on board. Stumbling on, he came toward the lock, with lights trained on it and people standing about.

That's when Poppa felt a sudden, brutal push on the small of his back. As he tumbled to the water below, his mind raced with the terror of a man who cannot swim.

At breakfast the next morning—Tuesday—we were told that Poppa was taking his breakfast in bed after his ordeal of the night before. Stephen assured us that Poppa had never been in any actual danger of drowning. The canal was at most only five or six feet deep, and with so many people close by, almost anyone could have rescued him.

The real danger to Poppa, we realized, was the possible effect of the shock on his already-weakened heart. Thus we were relieved to learn, when Molly came up to the salon for breakfast, that Poppa had slept peacefully through the night and seemed surprisingly unaffected by the whole experience, except for his stubborn insistence that he had been pushed when he fell into the canal.

"Poppa is obsessed with the idea that someone pushed him," she said. "I have tried to assure him that he probably had one of his dizzy spells and simply fell, but he becomes very agitated if I insist. So I wonder if all of you will simply go along with him on this. If he tells you he was pushed, don't try to reason with him!"

Everyone murmured their assent.

12

After breakfast Poppa, fully dressed and looking rosy and none the worse for his ordeal of the night before, came up on deck to go on with our tape sessions.

"Let's go!" he insisted. "I'm feeling fine!"

Marie appeared at his elbow. "Would you like some decaf coffee, Monsieur?"

Poppa beamed at her. "Yes, dear, thank you!"

As she poured his cup, Poppa looked archly at Andrew and me, then, adopting a piteous tone, said to the girl, "Well, Marie, somebody pushed me last night when I fell in the canal. What do you think of that?"

Marie, who had heard Molly's caution about contradicting Poppa on this subject, adopted a serious expression. "It is terrible!"

"Why would anyone want to do that?"

"I don't know, Monsieur. I am sure everyone likes you."

"Yes. Well, it looks as if somebody *doesn't* like me, wouldn't you say?"

"I am sure I don't know." Marie smiled demurely. "Is there anything else I can get for you, Monsieur?"

"No, sweetheart, that's all for now." And Poppa sighed but said nothing further on the subject for the moment.

The boat had left the canal and was moving now along the river Saône, with its tree-lined grassy banks and vistas of green fields and rolling hills. Throughout the morning, voices could be heard in a kind of counterpoint.

Ellen said to Don: "Not quite so warm today. I think I'll sit here on the deck and read."

Rosanna and Tonio vocalized in their cabins, their voices rising and falling in their daily scales and exercises.

Poppa was saying: "When we came to California, it was Harry who got us into real estate. The agency has made plenty of money, but we really hit the boom in California property and rode up with it. Harry invested right along with me and we both made a packet."

Julie's voice, from the piano, rose in exasperation: "Karl, Beethoven may have been deaf as a post when he wrote this, but he could hear inside his head. He knew what he wanted in this passage and he did *not* want to hear repeated notes on the violin at double forte. He wanted to hear *this*—" And she played the theme that belonged to the piano at that point in the music.

Karl growled: "All right, all right—but *you* keep under when *I* have the theme."

Later, when Rosanna and Tonio came above, I watched with amusement as Rosanna planted herself by the piano and looked Karl in the eye: "We'll take the piano when you are ready."

Karl's automatic flash of indignation wilted under her gaze. "Of course. Five minutes, yes?"

This time Rosanna played the piano herself as she and Tonio worked on some passages in the first act of *Bohème,* again shaping each phrase to bring out the dramatic effect.

Presently, when Andrew and I paused in our interview with Poppa, Rosanna spoke out loudly enough for Poppa to hear. "Of course it will depend on who's conducting at Glyndebourne."

Smoothly, Poppa raised his voice in reply: "One of the big problems in this line of work is that the talent are so damned unreasonable. Temperamental is not the word. Sometimes they just want their own way, common sense or not!"

Rosanna allowed Poppa's remark to hang in the air, then returned to the music with ostentatious indifference.

Poppa, ignoring Rosanna in turn, now began to tell us a number of anecdotes about celebrated performers he had known.

"Here's one you can use for sure, because the people are all dead now. It was one day in New York. Mr. X"—he named a world-famous pianist—"sometimes liked to have a little 'company' on those long concert tours, but this time, when they got to the Waldorf-Astoria, his wife decided to arrive from Paris and surprise him. Our man Joe, who was detailed to his highness when he was in the States, had just come into the lobby when he saw the wife sweep up to the desk.

" 'Louise!' Joe sang out as if overjoyed to see her. He knew X's little friend was upstairs in the suite and for a moment he panicked. Then he remembered that in the pocket of his topcoat he had a tuning fork.

" 'Look, dear, I think the piano tuner is up there. Shall I ring up—?''

''Louise said, 'No, darling, I'll just go straight up.' Fortunately, some friends arrived and surrounded her. While they exchanged the usual kisses and chitchat, Joe skimmed up the stairs to the third floor, praying the two were not actually in bed. When X answered the door fully dressed, Joe breathed a big sigh of relief, grabbed the girlfriend, and handed her the tuning fork.

''When Louise arrived, she heard the familiar ping of the tuner and paid no attention to the young woman bent over the piano. All's well that ends well.''

Poppa chuckled. ''Then there was the tenor who meant to take an upper before the performance and accidentally took a sleeping pill instead. The critics all remarked on his unusually mellow tone that evening!''

Shortly before one o'clock we broke for lunch. When the entire group had assembled in the salon, Poppa evidently decided the moment had come for a bit of drama.

''Now that I have you all together,'' he began, ''I want to tell you something.''

Faces turned toward Poppa and silence fell over the group.

''I am going to have my lunch downstairs. I'm pretty tired. But before I go, I have something to say. You may not know this, but last night I didn't fall into the canal by accident. Somebody pushed me!''

Instead of the chorus of protest he expected, Poppa found his announcement greeted with silence. ''Oh, I see. Molly has probably told you to humor me, right? Well, let me tell you this: I didn't imagine it—I ought to know. I felt a shove right in the middle of my back and in I went. All I have to say is, if anybody has it in for me''—and here he looked straight at Rosanna—

"they better not try any more tricks. It may have been meant for a joke, but with my heart, it might not be so funny. Just keep that in mind!"

Poppa turned as if to go, then paused theatrically. "And I'll tell you something else. Don't think you can get by with anything, because Andrew here is a good detective. His agent told me he solved a murder last year when the police were stuck. He's a regular Sherlock Holmes!"

And with this salvo, Poppa turned and went down the stairs.

Andrew looked painfully embarrassed at the chorus of questions that naturally followed Poppa's remark. "I had plenty of help from Jane here," he said diffidently. "I can't take all the credit."

We both protested that our talents had been greatly exaggerated and soon managed to change the subject.

Rosanna then loudly proclaimed to everyone that whatever Poppa thought, she certainly had not shoved him into the canal. "Tempting though it might be," she added with a grim smile. After much discussion everyone agreed that Poppa's fall had indeed been an accident.

After lunch everyone but Poppa went on the minibus for a tour of an elegant old château and then to a vineyard, where we sampled a fine white wine that had recently been awarded the coveted designation of Appellation Controlée. Meanwhile, the *Jacqueline* had continued along the river to the town of Chalon, where the bus deposited us after the tour.

Dinner that evening passed pleasantly. Poppa stayed up and talked with his guests for more than an hour. Rested and in good spirits, he joked and laughed but made no further reference to his fall into the canal. He and Rosanna appeared to have tacitly agreed to a truce. We heard him tell her that the office had had no further contact with the people at Glyndebourne that day, and she seemed willing to await developments.

The dramatic event of the evening came as Ellen and I lay in our beds reading before turning out the lights. We heard a tap on the door and Molly came in, her lovely brown eyes smiling.

"Such good news, girls. I persuaded Poppa to make the will!"

Ellen sat up. "Momma! How did you do it?"

"Well, when Poppa was ready for bed, I just looked him in the eye and said, 'All right, Poppa, no more nonsense. If someone really did push you into the canal, it means there might be another attempt on your life.'

"Poppa tried to look solemn, but his eyes were dancing. I knew he couldn't resist the drama of the situation.

"So I handed him a large pad of paper and a pen, and I said, 'So, you see, you must make a will right now so that we have something to go on before you get back to California and see the lawyer. I have written this out for you to copy.'

"For a minute he looked absolutely furious. Then he gave me a really sweet smile and said, 'Okay, Doll, you're right. I'll do whatever you say. But will this be legal?'

"I explained to him that it's called a holographic will. It must be all in his handwriting, on unlined paper, dated and signed, and it's just as binding as one drawn by a lawyer. I told him to read what I had written first and see if it's what he wanted, and he said it was fine and copied it all out like a lamb. See, girls, here's what I wrote."

Molly was holding a pad of yellow paper, from which she read out to us what she had written on the top sheet. The will, simply stated, left all of Poppa's property, both real and personal, to his wife, Margaret Hubbard O'Connor, for her lifetime. "That's called a life estate," Molly explained. "I can use the income but the principal goes to the children." After Molly's death the estate would be distributed in equal parts among (1) any living heirs of the body, (2) Donald Edward Hubbard, and (3) Ellen Hubbard Walker.

"You see, Ellie, it's the same as if Poppa had three children. This way his son by Odette is protected, along with you and Don."

Molly smiled. "I feel so relieved. I won't need this anymore." She tore off the yellow sheet, folded it, and dropped it into our miniscule wastebasket.

"I've already mailed Poppa's copy. As I told him, I've sent it to Harry tonight to keep in the office safe until we get back. I had some stamps, so I took it to the mailbox up by the bridge. Now if anything happens to me, it's all right."

Ellen and I smiled with her. No one expected then that anything would happen to Molly.

13

By lunchtime on Wednesday the *Jacqueline* had moved along the river to the charming little town of Tournus, with its ancient Abbey of St. Philibert.

We spent the afternoon visiting the Abbey and wandering about the town, our groups vaguely forming and dispersing. In the late afternoon Molly went back to the boat to find Poppa unconscious in his bed. An ambulance came and Poppa was taken to the small hospital at the top of the hill above the town.

For more than an hour the local doctors worked over Poppa, while a call was placed for a heart specialist to come from Lyon. Ellen and I sat with Molly and Don in the small waiting room while the others, including members of the crew, came and went, inquiring solicitously for news. Only Karl and Julie were absent, having already departed for their concert in Lyon that evening. They had elected to drive rather than take the train, and accordingly Poppa had arranged for a rental car for them.

"If we drive," Karl had pointed out, "we can return

afterward to the boat. Otherwise we would have to stay over in Lyon for the night.''

By half past six in the evening, there was no change in Poppa's condition, and Molly urged all of us to go back to the boat for dinner.

"There's nothing you can do here," she said, adding with a wan smile, "No use wasting one of Philippe's marvelous meals.''

"Go on, sis," said Don. "I'll stay with Momma. We can send out for sandwiches.''

After some urging, Ellen agreed and we started off down the hill.

Ellen said, "I think Momma is better off without everyone hanging around. Don is so calm. He'll be good for her.''

Dinner was a somber and hurried affair for those of us who were left. No one had changed. Even Rosanna and Tonio appeared in casual pants and sweaters.

When the meal was over, we all set out to walk up the hill toward the hospital. A cold wind had come up, and Andrew looked ruefully at his sweater. "This isn't enough," he said. "I'm going back for a jacket.''

When he caught up with us a few minutes later, Rosanna and Tonio had gone on ahead and Andrew fell in beside Ellen and me, saying with amusement, "I just stumbled on a touching scene between Romeo and Juliet.''

We smiled. Everyone on board knew by this time that Emile and Marie were lovers.

"What happened?" Ellen asked.

"I came out of my cabin, pulling on my jacket, and started up the stairs when I heard their voices on the deck. They thought we had all gone. My French isn't as good as Jane's, but I got the gist of it. Emile sounded furious. He said, 'Where do you think you're going?'

"Marie shrieked, 'Let go. You're hurting me!' and Emile sort of growled. Then her voice turned all sweetness and she said, 'I told you. I'm going up to ask about poor Mr. O'Connor.'

"Our hero said, 'Oh, yeah? You don't give a shit about Mr. O'Connor. You're going to meet that guy on the motorcycle again.'

"Marie sounded really startled. She said, 'What do you mean?' and he snarled again. 'You thought I didn't know. Well, I do. I saw you talking to him the other day and I didn't say anything. But when I saw you meeting him again this afternoon, right here in Tournus—well, dammit, that's too much!'

"Marie murmured something I couldn't hear. I stood there thinking what to do. If I came above now, they would know they'd been overheard. Not that it would really matter, but I didn't want to embarrass the girl. I had just decided to go back and close the door of my cabin loudly, then come out whistling, when I heard the sound of a blow and a cry of real pain from Marie.

"I leapt toward the top of the stairs, Sir Lancelot ready to defend the maiden in distress, when suddenly all was quiet and there they were, wrapped around each other and needing no help from the outside world. I retreated down the steps, began whistling loudly, and when I came back up, the deck was empty."

We laughed. Ellen asked, "What's all this about some man on a motorcycle?"

Then I told them about seeing Marie on Monday meeting with the mustached fellow on the Honda.

Ellen grinned. "Quite the tricky little wench, isn't she? I would think Emile would be enough for her!"

* * *

Back at the hospital Don reported no change in Poppa's condition.

"Momma is sitting with him," he told us. "She's very upset. We assumed Poppa had had a heart attack, but the doctors say now that he had an overdose of his afternoon medicine. I know Momma is blaming herself for not having watched him more closely."

Ellen protested. "But after all, Poppa isn't a child. He should be able to count his tablets as well as anyone else."

"But of course, that is right," Tonio said.

"Absolutely," Rosanna agreed. "Molly is a dear, but she has always spoiled him." Then she turned to Don.

"May I see him?"

Don reached out and patted her hand. "Sure. In fact, you can all go in. He's still unconscious."

Walking softly, we followed Don down the corridor and through a door on the right. Poppa lay on his back, his face ashen, the mouth slack. A tube from a hanging bottle led to an IV taped to his arm. Lines from his chest connected to a monitor that beeped softly as it traced his heartbeats.

Molly sat on one side of the bed and a nurse stood opposite, writing on a chart. Molly looked up at Rosanna, her eyes filling with tears, and the two women embraced.

Rosanna looked down again at the figure in the bed. "Poor old Poppa," she said quietly.

After a moment we filed silently out and Molly followed us into the corridor, where Don stood waiting.

"Look, Momma," Don said, "let me sit with him for a while. Why don't you go out for a walk? Get some fresh air. There's nothing you can do here."

"He's right, Molly," Rosanna said. "Come on."

Molly paused for a moment, then turned to Don. "All right, dear, thank you. I'll do that."

"I brought your warm coat, Momma," Ellen said. "There's a cold wind out there."

"Let's all go," Rosanna said, and the rest of us followed Molly and Ellen out the door of the hospital.

The sun had set but it was still light as we crossed the road and walked down the hill in the direction of the Abbey. As we approached the magnificent structure with its gray stone turrets and towers still standing since the twelfth century, we were surprised to see lights in the church and hear music coming from the interior.

"Oh, marvelous, there must be a service," exclaimed Rosanna. "Let's go in!"

As we entered at the west end of the Abbey, the air was filled with music from the organ and a chorus of voices. A small congregation was scattered among the chairs toward the front of the long central nave, looking very far away from where we stood.

We had all been through the Abbey at various times that afternoon. Now my heart lifted again at the grandeur of the ancient stone arches high above, the sight even more stirring with the music in our ears. I looked with pleasure at the grand simplicity of the immense pillars and the rounded Romanesque arches overhead, with their alternate banding of rose and white stone, from an era before the Gothic arch had been dreamed of.

Presently our group separated as each of us began wandering down the aisles on either side of the nave, where a handful of others—tourists like ourselves, no doubt—moved quietly along, looking into the side chapels and up into the lofty vaulting overhead.

I saw Molly, halfway down the left aisle, move toward the chairs which were set out in the central nave and sit down heavily, staring straight ahead as if in a daze.

A few minutes later, as the service came to a close, the music of the organ rolled out grandly. Now the visitors to the Abbey were able to walk into the central aisle and enjoy the vista of the full length of the great structure. As I stood with Ellen and Andrew near the altar, looking back down the length of the nave, Rosanna came up to join us.

"Marvelous, isn't it?" she said in her rich singer's voice. "Reminds me of St. Albans in England. When I was married to Sir Henry, he had a place in Hertfordshire not far from there." Rosanna chuckled. "He wanted us to be married at St. Albans, poor dear, but by that time I had been divorced twice already and it was no dice. The Church of England is pretty stuffy about divorce!"

Now Ellen looked at Rosanna and smiled. "Where's Tonio?"

"Oh, I think he went off to light a candle. Praying for his sins, no doubt." Rosanna's laugh gurgled up from her diaphragm and she gave Andrew a provocative look with her enormous black eyes. Putting her hand on his arm, she said, "Come see this divine little chapel," and they moved away.

Ellen looked at me. "My God, Jane, it must be marvelous to take life so casually. Will I ever be able to laugh about my divorce? I wish I could be like that. Ever since I was a kid I've seen Rosanna sail blithely through a series of marriages, divorces, and assorted lovers. Sometimes she was angry or involved in dramatic recriminations or legal tangles, but she never seemed to suffer real anguish."

"I know what you mean," I said. "Do you think this relationship with Tonio is different? Maybe under that casual manner a fierce passion is burning."

"I've wondered about that too. She's not getting any younger."

As Andrew and Rosanna came back, Tonio´ came hurrying up to join them, his handsome face slightly flushed. "Sorry to keep you waiting," he murmured.

Rosanna dropped Andrew's arm and turned her full gaze on Tonio. "It's all right, darling."

Suddenly Ellen looked back down the nave. "Where's Momma?"

We all stopped and looked around in surprise. It was unlike Molly to wander off.

Andrew said, "Perhaps she's gone out. I'll look outside."

Rosanna turned to Tonio. "She might have gone to that chapel upstairs. Why don't you go and look?"

"Yes, of course."

Ellen said to Rosanna, "You take the right aisle. Jane, let's go down this way," and she began walking briskly down the left aisle.

Andrew told us afterward that when he stepped through the outer door into the square, a handful of people were still coming out of the Abbey. By now darkness had fallen and he stood for a moment while his eyes grew accustomed to the dim light. He saw no sign of Molly but suddenly he heard a voice shout *"Tiens!"* and our captain, Emile, ran past him toward a slim figure who was mounting a motorbike. Before Emile could reach his quarry, the cycle's motor roared and the rider flashed past and down the hill out of sight, giving Andrew a glimpse of a dark mustache and a stocking cap.

Emile clenched his fist and muttered what Andrew recognized as a series of oaths, of which *"Merde!"* was the least offensive. So this was the fellow Marie had been meeting, Andrew said to himself. I hope he can defend himself if Emile catches up with him!

Seeing no sign of Molly, Andrew turned to go back into the church when he saw Stephen Shaw near the door and asked if he had seen Mrs. O'Connor. Stephen shook his head. "No. Isn't she at the hospital? I was coming along to inquire when I heard the service here at the church and stopped in to listen. How is Mr. O'Connor?"

"There was no change when we left half an hour or so ago. If you see Mrs. O'Connor, will you tell her we're ready to go back to the hospital?"

"Yes, of course."

Andrew watched as Stephen walked away, then turned back toward the church.

Meanwhile Tonio hurried up the narrow circular staircase that led to the ancient chapel above the narthex, with its massive pillars and medieval simplicity. A quick glance at the barren emptiness of the chapel was sufficient to see that Molly was not there, and he made his way painfully down the steep and twisting stairs.

Ellen and I had moved quickly down the aisle and were about to enter the ambulatory when a verger came toward us, crying, *"C'est fermé"* and motioning us to leave.

I asked if he had seen a lady for whom we were looking.

"No, Madame, no one is here."

Turning back, we saw the stone stairs leading down to the crypt. No one had signaled that Molly had been found, and we were sure she wouldn't have gone back to the hospital without letting us know. We agreed that if Molly had gone down into the crypt, she might not have been able to hear that the service had ended.

We started down the short flight of steps when the verger cried out again that the church was closing and we must leave. Ignoring him, we reached the bottom of the stairs and stepped into the gloom of the dimly lighted crypt.

"Momma!" Ellen called.

Only a faint echo of her voice came back to us.

The ancient stone pillars seemed to rise up out of the darkness as we moved slowly along, feeling our way past the cold and barren walls. Walking farther into the central aisle, Ellen called again: "Momma, are you here?"

Then we heard the verger behind us, protesting that we must go. Turning with a sigh, Ellen began to move toward the stairs when we heard a faint moaning sound that seemed to come straight out of the wall at our right.

"Momma, are you there?" Ellen called.

Again we heard the low moaning from the wall, and now we remembered.

"The little chapels!" Ellen cried.

That afternoon we had explored the crypt and noticed the narrow entrances along the wall. After a step up, a little chapel, no bigger than a cell, could be seen to the right or the left, but each was quite invisible from the main floor of the crypt. Perhaps each chapel had once contained an altar rich with hangings and gilded vessels, suitably enshrined, but now they were empty, the barren stone making them seem more like prison cells than places of worship.

Quickly I stepped up into the aperture nearest me and found the cell empty, while Ellen, almost stumbling in her haste, tried the next opening.

"Not here," I called, and Ellen answered, "This one's empty."

Ellen ran to the next opening in the wall and I heard her cry out, "She's here!"

Looking over Ellen's shoulder, I could just make out in the darkness a huddled form lying on the floor.

Ellen dropped to her knees. "Oh, Momma, what happened?"

Again we heard only the faint moan.

"It's all right, Momma darling. We'll get help!"

"Stay with her," I said, and flew up the stairs, calling to the others.

After that everything moved rapidly. Andrew ran up the hill to the hospital, and the same ambulance that had come for Poppa that afternoon brought Molly back to the hospital.

It was only afterward that Ellen remembered that the verger, now deeply concerned, had held his flashlight to dispel the darkness of the tiny chapel where Molly lay, and on the bare stone floor lay a heavy brass candlestick, the tip still red with blood.

An hour later Molly had been treated by the doctors and placed in a room just two doors away from where Poppa lay in a coma. Ellen, pale and distraught, sat by her mother's bed, clutching my hand. Don moved back and forth between the two rooms, making an occasional report to those in the waiting room.

We were all stunned by the fact that someone had evidently made an attempt on Molly's life. Although Molly had regained consciousness, she was still in a state of considerable mental confusion.

As the law required, the local doctor had informed the police of the attack on Molly, and a uniformed officer had come to the hospital to obtain the facts for his report. Molly had been able to murmur yes or no to his questions, establishing that she had no idea who her attacker might be. Then the doctor suggested that further questioning be deferred until the morning.

Sometime after ten o'clock Don came to the door of his mother's room and stood quietly looking at Ellen. Don saw that Molly's eyes were closed, and looking toward Poppa's room and back at Ellen, he shook his head. Ellen caught her breath and as Don put his fingers to his lips in a signal not to let Molly hear, her eyes opened and she looked from one to the other.

"It's Poppa, isn't it?" she whispered.

Ellen murmured "Yes" and Don took his mother's hand. "He's gone, Momma," he said, his voice breaking.

Then Molly closed her eyes and we saw two tears well up under her eyelids and slide down her cheeks and onto the pillow.

14

The next morning at breakfast we were a pretty gloomy group and the weather matched our mood. It had rained in the night and the sky was a patchwork of clouds, some gray, some white.

Karl and Julie had learned about Poppa's death and the attack on Molly when they returned about midnight from their recital in Lyon.

No one seemed very hungry, but we had all taken something from the buffet and were sitting at the dining tables in the salon when Stephen announced that the police had arrived.

"Ladies and gentlemen, may I present Inspecteur Moreau of the Police Judiciaire." I saw a slender man, thirtyish, of medium height, in a dark suit and tie, with a long, narrow face, brown eyes, and a thick, dark mustache.

"*Mesdames et messieurs,* good morning. My English is not very good. Please to forgive."

The inspector's eyes moved over the assembled

group and suddenly his face was alight. "Andrew! *Quelle surprise!*"

"Bernard!" Andrew leapt to his feet and the two men embraced in the French fashion, touching both cheeks, then conversed in a confused mixture of French and English.

Andrew turned to the assembled group. "Bernard— I should say Inspector Moreau—and I have been friends since he visited the States some time ago. Now he is attached to the detective branch in Lyon and was called here by the local police to investigate the attack last night on Mrs. O'Connor. He tells me that it's also necessary for the police to officially determine the cause of Mr. O'Connor's death."

So, I thought, I must stop making jokes, because, as I had whimsically predicted, here was Andrew's detective friend from the Police Judiciare to investigate both a crime and a death.

Stephen Shaw looked startled. "But we assumed— I mean, surely, the death of Mr. O'Connor was owing to an accidental overdose of his medicine?" He turned to the inspector. *"C'est vrai, n'est-ce pas?"*

"But it must be proved to the satisfaction of the police." The inspector smiled slightly. "Is it not so in England and in America?"

"Oh, of course. Yes, indeed." Stephen nodded. "I merely meant that we should not like our guests on Euro-Cruises to be subjected to unpleasantness."

The inspector introduced the uniformed officer who accompanied him as Brigadier Dupuis, a rank I learned was roughly equivalent to that of sergeant.

Moreau said, "I should like to speak to each of you, if I may. If Monsieur Shaw will call each person?"

Both officers took out their notebooks and sat at a table in the salon. Then the inspector addressed Andrew. "And perhaps Monsieur Quentin will assist me with the translation?"

Andrew laughed. "Actually, Jane would be much better at that than I would. She lived here in France for a year as a student."

Accordingly, I was introduced to the inspector and duly installed at his side as unofficial translator.

When Andrew started to leave, Inspector Moreau smiled. "No, Andrew, you remain, please. I have heard of your activities as amateur detective. We shall consult!"

Andrew grinned back and took a place at the table, while Marie brought coffee for all of us.

When the others had withdrawn to the sun deck or to their cabins below, the inspector asked Stephen Shaw for a list of everyone on board, including the members of the crew. Stephen stepped behind the bar and returned with a sheet of paper which he handed to the inspector. "Here is a copy of the guest list. I shall bring you a list of the crew members."

Looking over the list, the inspector asked for clarification, and Andrew briefly identified each person, including ourselves.

"I believe we will begin with the members of the family," said the inspector.

When Stephen returned with the list of the crew, the inspector slipped it under the list of the guests in front of him. Then he said to Stephen, "May we have Monsieur Hubbard, please," pronouncing the name "Oo-bar."

Don Hubbard came in and took a seat at the table, bringing his coffee cup with him.

While rendered here in English, the interviews that followed were conducted in a mixture of languages. The crew members, of course, spoke in French. For the others, whose French was limited, the inspector spoke in both languages, with some help from me. Then, when necessary, I repeated the answers in French for Dupuis, who wrote rapidly in his notebook.

Thus began the series of interviews which we all thought at the time would be finished within an hour or two but which in the end occupied the whole of that day.

Inspector Moreau began. "Monsieur Hubbard, may I express to you my sympathy for the death of Mr. O'Connor and for the—er—injury to your mother?"

Don's frank, open face clouded over. "Thank you very much, Inspector. As I told the others at breakfast, I visited my mother early this morning and she is feeling much better."

"Yes, I understand from the doctors that her mind is clearer this morning, and I shall wish to talk with her later today."

"When I saw her this morning, she told me she had no idea who could have attacked her at the Abbey last night. All she remembers is that the person called her by name."

"Precisely. That is the information that I have also in the police report from this morning. Now, Monsieur Hubbard, can you suggest a reason why anyone known to you would wish to kill your mother—for I am afraid that from the nature of the attack we must conclude that that was probably the intention."

Don shuddered. "No, no, it's impossible. Mother is the sweetest, dearest—everyone loves her. It must have been a stranger, perhaps hoping to find money in her purse."

"Are you aware that the police found over ten thousand francs in Mrs. O'Connor's handbag when they examined it at the hospital?"

"No. In fact, I have to admit I've been too upset to

think about it logically. Well, maybe the person heard someone coming and ran off.''

"Yes, that is certainly possible. But a stranger would not know your mother's name, surely?''

"He could have heard someone in our party calling her by name.''

"Yes, perhaps.''

The inspector turned to his assistant. "Are we going too fast for you?''

"No, Monsieur.'' Dupuis gave an impish grin in my direction. "As one says in America, 'No problem!' ''

Everyone smiled, and the tension relaxed.

"Now, Monsieur Hubbard, I understand that at the time of the attack on your mother, you were in the hospital at the bedside of your stepfather?''

"Yes.''

"Very well. Then let us turn to the afternoon of yesterday. What can you tell me about Mr. O'Connor and the taking of his medicine?''

"Well, Poppa—everyone calls him Poppa—''

"I see. Thank you.''

"Poppa had had a heart attack two years or so ago and another one more recently. The doctor gave him medicine which he usually took before his rest in the afternoon and again at bedtime.''

"Did he take the medicine faithfully?''

"Oh, yes, Momma made sure of that.''

"Of course we do not have the report of the autopsy as yet—''

Don looked startled. "You mean there will be an autopsy?''

"Oh, certainly. In all cases of death in unexplained circumstances, it is required.''

"I see. I guess we all thought it was obvious that he just made a mistake and took more than the usual amount.''

"Was Mr. O'Connor aware of the danger of ingesting more than the prescribed amount of the medicine?"

"Yes, he was. That's why we were so surprised he wasn't more careful—" Don stopped abruptly.

"Precisely." The inspector turned over the page of the tablet on which he was making brief notations.

"Now, Monsieur Hubbard, were other members of your party also aware of the danger that might ensue from an overdose of the medicine?"

"Probably everybody had heard some mention of it. It was certainly no secret."

"Could the members of the crew also have this knowledge?"

Don smiled wryly. "On a boat as small as this, I should imagine they hear a good deal. I don't mean intentionally—"

"Yes, I understand." The inspector peered into his empty coffee cup and looked at his assistant, who brought the pot from the dining area and refilled the cups.

When we were settled again, the inspector continued. "Monsieur Hubbard, can you describe to me where Monsieur O'Connor's medicine was kept?"

"Yes. I believe the bottle containing the tablets was usually standing on his bedside table."

"Did he have a glass of water available when he took the tablets?"

"No, he usually took them with a glass of wine. It helped him to get to sleep. In fact, he usually drank another glass before dropping off for his afternoon nap. Sometimes he would nod off, then open his eyes and take the second glass while he was half asleep."

"In a moment I shall want to examine the cabin of Monsieur and Madame O'Connor. First, however, I should like to know if anyone had a motive for wishing to—shall we say?—dispose of Monsieur O'Connor?''

Don sighed. ''I may as well tell you the whole story because it will all come out, anyway, by the time you've talked to everyone else.''

The inspector looked impassive. ''Yes, please.''

''Well, I suppose you could say that before yesterday, my sister and I had what you would call a 'motive' for getting rid of Poppa, except that it's ridiculous because we would never do anything like that.''

I saw Andrew flinch slightly at Don's blithe admission, then decided that maybe Don's frankness would make a favorable impression on the inspector.

''You see,'' Don went on, ''Poppa was married many years ago to a French lady named Odette. She left him and got a divorce, and about a year later Poppa met my mother and they were married. My own father had died the year before when my sister and I were only two and four years old. Momma wanted Poppa to adopt us, but he never did.''

''Why did he not do so?''

Don looked troubled. ''Honestly, I don't know. He was always good to us and he took me into the business after college. Sometimes Poppa was just—well, he could be totally stubborn if anybody tried to urge him to do something.''

''Then what was the circumstance which would cause you and your sister to be—er—angry with Monsieur Poppa?''

''We weren't really angry with him. It was more that we would have had a reason to be.''

Don heaved a sigh, then struggled on, trying to find the right words. ''When we were in Paris last Saturday night, Poppa's former wife, Odette, called him on the phone—she lives in Paris now—and told him she was pregnant when she left him and that Poppa had a son who would now be about twenty-five years old, I guess. Then Momma told Poppa he should make a will so that his own son could not inherit a lot of his property and leave Ellen and me out of the picture. We told Momma we didn't care, but anyway it didn't matter because on Tuesday night Poppa did make a will, putting all three of us in, and Momma mailed it to his office in Los Angeles. So, you see, it was settled after all.''

"I see. And did others in the party know about all this?''

"Yes, I'm afraid so. It was the talk of the boat!''

"And where is the son of Madame Odette now?''

Don shook his head. "We don't know. Poppa was to meet him when we got back to Paris." Suddenly tears came to Don's eyes and he tried to blink them away. "Oh, God, I still can't take it in—that Poppa is gone. Poor old guy—it's awful!''

The inspector stood up. "Thank you, Monsieur Hubbard. You have been most helpful. I believe now that we should examine the cabin of your parents. Will you lead the way?''

15

In the O'Connors' cabin, we stood at the foot of the bed while the police officers examined the room. The bed was still unmade, as the inspector had taken the routine precaution when he first boarded the boat of asking that the cabin remain undisturbed.

Now he studied the bedside table, with its glowing ruby glass decanter and wineglass, and the plastic medicine bottle. A magazine lay on the floor, where it might have fallen from Poppa's hand when he fell asleep or might have been pushed aside when the ambulance attendants had placed him on a stretcher.

A cordless extension phone lay on the table, its antenna extended.

"You have telephone service here?"

Don cleared his throat. "At certain locations the captain can make a connection with the telephone service. The main connection is in the salon above and Poppa used the extension phone here in his cabin."

The inspector's eyes fell upon a second wineglass on the other bedside table.

"Your mother's?"

"Yes. Momma had a regular routine at home as well as when they traveled. My sister and I have seen it many times. Momma would open the wine bottle, let it stand for a while, then pour wine for both of them, putting the remainder into the decanter by Poppa's bedside. If he was ready for his medicine then, she would count out two tablets and he would take them with his wine. Before actually falling asleep, I believe he would usually finish off the rest of the wine."

"I see. And if your Poppa was not ready for his medicine?"

"Then Momma prepared everything for him before she left the room."

"Do you know if she would lock the door of the cabin here before leaving?"

"No. In fact, there are no locks on the doors. Just a little bolt you can turn when you are inside."

"So anyone could have access to the Poppa's cabin?"

"Oh, yes, I suppose so."

The inspector bent over and peered into the wineglass and the decanter on Poppa's table. "Dupuis!"

Without further instruction the officer stepped briskly forward and brought out several plastic bags from a canvas kit, like a magician producing rabbits out of a hat. Handling the objects with great care, the sergeant placed decanter, glass, and medicine bottle in separate bags, pressing the top of each to form a seal, then stowed them in the canvas bag.

The inspector nodded to his assistant, who disappeared up the stairs. "We should have a preliminary report on these this afternoon."

Back in the salon, Andrew and I sat with the inspector at the table again while Don joined the other members of the party out on the deck, where pale sunshine was beginning to disperse the early morning clouds.

Speaking in a low voice, the inspector said, "So, what have we now? I thought this would be merely a routine inquiry, but many possibilities arise, is it not so?"

Andrew looked directly at his friend. "Before we go any further, Bernard, I should say that if you believe that a number of people had the opportunity to tamper with Poppa O'Connor's medicine or to attack Mrs. O'Connor last night, then you must see that Jane and I may also be suspects."

The inspector laid his hand on Andrew's arm, and his eyes grew serious. "No, my friend, it is clear that you have no personal connection with the people here, and you have vouched for the character of Madame Jane. If evidence appears to cast suspicion on either of you, then we shall act accordingly. Meanwhile, I shall be glad to have you with me in this inquiry and to use the help of Madame with the language difficulties."

We both expressed our thanks, and Inspector Moreau went on.

"So, Andrew, what is your opinion about the theory that Monsieur O'Connor took the extra tablets of medicine by mistake?"

"I've thought a lot about that. It is certainly possible that he might have taken the first two tablets, then become drowsy and, forgetting that he had already taken them, take several more. However, against that is the fact that he has been taking these routinely in the afternoon and at bedtime for several months and this has not happened before. More important, my impression of Poppa is that he might have been careless about a lot of things, but he would be extremely careful of his own safety. He was a good deal of an egotist, you see, and that kind of person has strong instincts for survival.''

"Yes, I see. Your answer would also appear to rule out the second possibility, which is that Monsieur O'Connor wished to take his own life. Madame Jane, you have known the family. What is your opinion?''

"I'm afraid that anyone who knew Poppa would never believe that he would commit suicide. It's true that anyone may behave uncharacteristically under pressure of circumstance, but in this case Poppa was not only cheerful and in good spirits, he was very excited about getting back to Paris on Saturday when his former wife had promised to telephone him again and introduce him to his son.''

"I see. Now, about the matter of Mr. O'Connor's son by his first wife—no one has met this young man, so far as is known?''

"That's correct.''

"Did not Madame Odette—the former wife—give her address?''

"Apparently not.''

The inspector lowered his voice again. "Then is it not possible that this young man may in some way have gained access to the boat and made away with Monsieur O'Connor? He may have nourished a hatred for him fostered by his mother, or, more likely, he may have hoped to inherit a great deal of money once his identity was established.''

Andrew nodded. "Yes, that's certainly possible.''

"But of course, it is obvious that a stranger could not know the location of the O'Connors' cabin nor the danger of the overdose of medicine. The man would have to be a member of the party, or he would have to be informed of the facts by someone who was on the boat.''

Andrew looked thoughtful. "Exactly. Following up on this, purely as hypothesis, there are several young men in their mid-twenties on the boat this week. The problem is that for any of these to be the unknown son would be an extraordinary coincidence.''

"My dear Andrew, if you had been in police work as long as I have, you would cease to be surprised at coincidence. However, it need not be so startling. Suppose, for example, that the coincidence occurs and that the son discovers that by chance he will be on this cruise. He may have no thought of committing a murder. He would perhaps welcome the chance to learn about his father without revealing his own identity.''

"Yes!" Andrew agreed. "And then, suddenly, the temptation is there. He has heard all the talk about making a will. First, Poppa has no will. Then he makes one providing for the son equally with the stepchildren. He is sure that it will appear to be an accident if Poppa takes an overdose of his medicine, and then it is only a matter of time until he inherits a packet of money. If he waits, Poppa might take a dislike to him or change his mind in the future about his will.''

The inspector studied the list of guests that Stephen Shaw had given him. "Which of these are of the right age?"

"Let's see. Tonio Riccardi, the tenor, and Karl Gebler, the violinist, are about that age.''

"And of the crew?"

"Yes, Stephen Shaw, the guide; Philippe, the chef; and the captain, Emile—I should think that all three are probably in their mid-twenties.''

"And what of the alternate theory—that someone

present on the boat could supply information to a person from the outside?''

''Oh, Lord!'' Andrew looked at me and the same thought came to both our minds.

''Of course,'' Andrew exclaimed, ''we just remembered. The mystery man on the motorcycle!''

16

Just as the inspector raised his eyebrows in inquiry at Andrew's exclamation, we heard voices on the deck and stepped out to see Ellen helping her mother up the gangplank. Don hurried forward and put Molly into a chair, where she sat down, looking extremely pale and dazed.

"I'm all right." Her voice was faint and uncertain.

"Don't try to talk, darling," Ellen said. To us, she explained: "The doctor released her and she came down in a taxi."

Everyone hovered around Molly, offering their condolences, while she nodded and tried to smile, her hand straying repeatedly to her bandaged head.

The inspector motioned us to return to the salon.

"I shall wish to speak with Mrs. O'Connor presently, but now she must rest. So, Andrew, what about this man of mystery on the motorbike?"

Andrew smiled. "The girl Marie and the captain apparently are lovers. I happened to overhear them yesterday. Emile was very angry because she has evidently been meeting some fellow who rides a motorcycle. Jane saw them on Monday.''

When I had described the scene I had witnessed, Andrew went on. ''Then last night, at the Abbey, I stepped outside to look for Mrs. O'Connor and saw Emile trying to flag down a chap on a Honda, but he rode off before Emile could reach him.''

''Did you see what he looked like?''

''It was dark, but I did get a glimpse of him—slight build, wearing a dark stocking cap, and sporting a little mustache. Obviously the same fellow Jane saw. He tore off down the hill in a hurry after he heard Emile shouting at him.''

The inspector began to draw circles and squares on his notepad. ''Where were the guests and the crew yesterday afternoon between luncheon and dinner?''

''The guests had a free afternoon to explore the area. The Abbey is, of course, only a five-minute walk up the hill, and everyone went there at one time or another. Some of us bicycled around the town, wandering through the shops and along the river.''

''And the crew?''

''I don't know, but from what Emile said to Marie, I assume that they must have been free to leave the boat, since he saw her meeting the man on the motorcycle somewhere here in Tournus.''

The inspector placed his circles and squares inside a large triangle and began shading in the spaces. ''You know, my friends, we may have a very serious situation here. I believe that I shall return to the police station and conduct the questioning there in a more official atmosphere. Can you come with me and we shall continue as before?''

''Yes, of course.''

The inspector rose to his feet. ''However, I shall

first ask to speak with Madame O'Connor and her daughter.''

Out on the deck, Molly sat in her chair, staring ahead of her like someone in a trance, but when Andrew gently asked her if she could answer a few questions for the inspector, she nodded her head mechanically. "I'm much better," she whispered.

The inspector took a chair beside Molly, and the rest of the party began to move tactfully into the salon.

Ellen asked, "May I stay?"

"But of course, Madame. We shall be only a moment.''

The inspector turned to Molly. "First, Madame O'Connor, can you tell me what took place after luncheon yesterday when you returned to your cabin?''

"Yes, of course. Poppa went down first and I followed a few minutes later." She looked at me. "You were with me, weren't you, Jane?''

"Yes, I was. Shall I tell him and let you rest?'' Molly nodded gratefully.

"Well then, as Mrs. O'Connor and I walked down the stairs, we were talking about the Los Angeles Philharmonic. Mrs. O'Connor had an article about the orchestra in a newsmagazine which I hadn't seen and she said, 'Come along and I'll find it for you.' When she opened the cabin door, Poppa was already on the phone.''

Molly and I exchanged glances. "As always," she said with a sad smile.

Ellen explained to the inspector. "Poppa called his office in Los Angeles almost every day. He liked to keep in touch, as he put it.''

"Anyhow," I went on, "there he was, talking to his business associate—something about a contract. He said, 'Just tear it up, Harry—' and then he saw us and said, 'Hi, Doll' and then into the phone, 'No, not you, Harry, it's Molly and Jane.' Molly was searching for the magazine for me, and Poppa went on talking to Harry, something about tearing up the contract and starting again.''

Ellen interposed. "Probably something to do with Rosanna and the fight over Glyndebourne."

The inspector looked puzzled and Ellen explained. "Rosanna Rossi is under contract to Poppa and has been for many years. She wanted him to get a certain part for her at next year's season at Glyndebourne in England, and Poppa had refused to put up a fight for her."

"Surely a great soprano like Madame Rossi can sing wherever she wishes?"

Ellen smiled slightly. "Yes, one would think so. But Glyndebourne wants a *young* singer for Mimi in *La Bohème.*"

The inspector's shoulders rose in an infinitesimal shrug. "Ah, yes," he said, "I understand."

"Anyhow," I went on, "Molly found the magazine under some pads of paper, so I left and didn't hear any more."

"Neither did I," Molly murmured. "Poppa hung up the phone just as you left."

The inspector readied his notebook. "Now, Madame O'Connor, can you tell me briefly what happened after Madame Jane left the cabin?"

"Yes. I opened a bottle of wine, poured out two glasses, and put the rest into the decanter. I went into the bathroom to freshen up. Then I came out and drank my own glass of wine. Poppa said he wanted to take his medicine a little later, so I told him good-bye"—Molly choked slightly, then went on—"and went up to join the others."

"And what was the time?"

"Oh, I should think a little after two o'clock."

"And who was present at that time?"

Ellen smiled and looked at Andrew. "We can answer that, can't we? Five of us called ourselves the Bicycle Club because we seem to be the only ones interested in biking. When Momma came up on deck, my brother Don and I, along with Jane and Andrew, and Julie—Miss Bergstrom—were getting out the bikes. We all decided to set off for the Abbey, and we walked our bikes up the quay and across the road by the bridge, with Momma walking along with us. Then we rode up and back and around her, the way children do when an adult is walking with them, all the way up the hill to the Abbey."

"Did you see anyone else from your party at that time?"

Ellen looked at Andrew. "I don't remember, do you?"

Andrew shook his head. "No, I can't say that I remember seeing any of the others just then."

The inspector looked inquiringly at Molly, who agreed. "No, no one."

Turning to a new page in his notebook, the inspector continued. "Madame O'Connor, turning to last evening, we have already learned that you believe your attacker called you by name. Can you tell me what was the name you heard?"

"Yes. It sounded like Molly but sort of drawn out, like Moll-eee."

"You were in the crypt when you heard the name spoken?"

"Yes. At the far end. I was leaning against a pillar."

"How did you happen to go down to the crypt, Madame?"

Molly put her hand to her head. "I really don't know. I was feeling very depressed. I think I wanted to get away from the lights and the people. I had been down there in the afternoon. It's dark and quiet there.''

''And what happened when you entered the crypt?''

''Nothing at first. I thought I heard footsteps coming down the stairs behind me, but no one came, so I thought I was mistaken. I started walking down toward the curved end of the crypt. It was even darker there. I remember leaning against a pillar and putting my cheek against the rough stone. I thought of all the pilgrims who had come there to pray for a thousand years. It's the oldest part of the Abbey, you know.

''Then I walked on, and I saw an altar, and I remember thinking there had been a bronze candlestick there in the afternoon, but I may have been wrong.''

Molly sighed.

Very gently, the inspector murmured, ''And then?''

''That was when I heard the sound. At first it was like a low humming. Then I heard the voice calling my name, 'Moll-eee.' ''

''Could you tell whether the voice was that of a man or a woman?''

''No, not at all. It was an eerie sound, sort of ghostlike.''

''Did you hear the sound more than once?''

''Yes, several times, I believe. When I moved closer, I thought it was coming out of the wall and I was frightened. Then I remembered the little chapels sort of hidden inside the walls and I thought it must be someone from our group calling me. But when I stepped up into the chapel, whoever it was must have slipped behind me and I felt a terrible blow on my head. I remember falling, falling—and that's all.'' Molly shuddered.

Ellen pressed her mother's hand.

The inspector asked, "Is there anything else you can remember?"

"No, I'm afraid not."

"Thank you, Madame. I am sorry to trouble you at such a time." The inspector rose and spoke to Ellen. "May I have a brief word with you, Madame Walker?"

"Of course."

Back in the salon, the inspector began: "Madame Walker, your brother has already described to me the circumstances leading to your stepfather's making a will to include yourself, your brother, and his own offspring. Can you tell me your feelings about this?"

"Yes. It was my mother who was concerned about the inheritance. Neither my brother nor I wanted to receive money from Poppa unless he wanted it that way himself. I earn enough to live very comfortably."

"But surely, Madame, additional money is always welcome, is it not?"

Ellen looked at the inspector with her forthright gaze, and a slight flush appeared on the fair skin of her cheeks. "Even if Poppa had not made a will, my mother would have had a fair amount of community property which would eventually come to us. I don't live in such expectation, but it is impossible not to be aware of it. Whatever that amount, it would provide a cushion of security for me, if that's what you mean."

Deftly the inspector shifted ground. "Did your stepfather have any enemies, so far as you know?"

Ellen smiled. "There were no doubt plenty of people in the world who disliked Poppa, but I don't think any of them are here on the cruise!"

"What of Madame Rossi? You spoke just now of a quarrel between them."

"Oh, that was nothing new. Poppa and Rosanna often squabbled about this and that, but it was never really serious. They both love to dramatize. Like that nonsense about Poppa being pushed into the canal."

Andrew started. "I'd forgotten about that!"

"So had I!" I said, startled out of my role as translator.

Ellen told the inspector about the incident of Poppa's fall into the canal on Monday evening, concluding with the remark, "Poppa clearly implied that Rosanna had pushed him, but no one believed it."

"I see. And now, turning to the events of last evening at the Abbey, can you tell me what you know of the attack on your mother?"

Ellen described our visit to the Abbey, our surprise at not seeing Molly when we were ready to leave, and her horror at finding her mother lying in the cell-like chapel in the crypt. She believed, as her brother did, that the attacker must have been a thief who was frightened away.

"Nothing else makes sense," she exclaimed. "Why should anyone want to kill Momma?"

17

Half an hour later Andrew and I were settled with Inspector Moreau in a room at the little police station in the town of Tournus, only a few minutes walk from the river, where the *Jacqueline* floated peacefully in the water.

As we walked up the hill toward the station, Andrew and the inspector had had their first chance to speak of their own lives. Moreau's first act was to express his sorrow over Norma's death, clasping Andrew in a spontaneous embrace. I was touched to see Andrew's usual reserve melt away at the Frenchman's voluble and sincere condolences. Tears sprang from his eyes and he wiped them away without embarrassment.

"You will come to us in Lyon as planned?" Moreau asked.

"Yes, of course. Whatever happens with this investigation, the cruise is at an end. I'll come as soon as it's possible."

Now Andrew inquired about Moreau's wife and

infant son, who was described to me as *"un enfant incomparable!"*

At the station Brigadier Dupuis reported that the objects taken from Poppa's cabin had been sent to the lab. Then he took a seat at the table, this time equipped with a tape recorder instead of his notebook.

Moreau telephoned the doctor who had been called in to assist and had treated Poppa at the hospital.

After listening and taking notes, he hung up the phone.

"He tells me there is no way to determine the precise time at which Monsieur O'Connor swallowed the overdose of his medicine. We know that he was at luncheon until shortly before two o'clock. His wife left him at a few minutes past two and returned at about half past four to find him in a coma.

"According to the doctor, an overdose of this kind would usually result in death very soon after its ingestion. Occasionally, as in this case, the patient survives for several hours in a coma, but the doctor cannot say precisely when the ingestion took place. It may have been any time between two o'clock and half past four."

"That leaves a wide-open field, I'm afraid," Andrew said.

"Exactly. So now we speak to the young lady, Marie."

"You won't need me for translation," I said. "Shall I step out?"

"No, my dear, you may as well remain. We can then, as you say in English, put our heads together, *n'est-ce pas?*"

A police officer had been sent to bring Marie to the station, and now she was ushered in and seated across the table.

"Your name, Mademoiselle?"

"Marie Dupont."

She gave an address in the Montparnasse district of Paris.

"And you work as a stewardess for the Euro-Cruises company?"

"No. I work in Paris at an insurance company. I am merely filling in this week because the stewardess became ill."

Andrew explained to the inspector about the original stewardess and her departure for the hospital on Sunday afternoon, just as the cruise began.

"So how is it that you are here, Mademoiselle?"

Marie smiled provocatively. "On Sunday afternoon I happened to be looking at the boat—the *Jacqueline*—and I met the captain, Emile. That evening he told me what had happened to the stewardess. Since I had worked on a hotel barge last summer for the same company, Emile spoke to Stephen Shaw, the tour guide, and they called the company and arranged for me to fill in this week."

"How did you happen to be in Burgundy just now?"

"I have two weeks free and I came down to bicycle with a girlfriend in Dijon, but she had sprained her ankle, so I went on by myself."

"May we please have the name and address of your friend in Dijon?"

For the first time, Marie hesitated. Her answers had been glib and confident, but now she paused. Then her ponytail flipped as she tossed her head. "I don't see why that is necessary."

The inspector's voice was quiet. "It is possible, Mademoiselle, that we are investigating a murder. Every detail is important."

Marie's eyes flew open and she caught her breath. Then she lowered her eyes. "My friend's name is

Jeanne Touche. I don't remember her address, but I can show you where she lives."

The inspector's eyebrows rose, but he did not pursue the question. Instead, he looked at Marie sternly. "Now, Mademoiselle, you will please tell us who is the young man on the motorcycle whom you have been meeting."

Marie tossed her head again and looked back at the inspector boldly. "Yes. He is a friend from Paris."

"His name, please."

"I do not wish to give his name. I swear to you that he has nothing to do with any of this."

"No, Mademoiselle, that will not do."

"Look, I will tell you the truth. He has been in trouble with the police in the past and he does not want to be involved in any questioning."

"Where is he now?"

Marie's mouth curved up in her little half smile. "He has gone back to Paris."

"Very well, Mademoiselle. You may be sure that we shall find him if we need to. Meanwhile, are you aware that if this young man is involved in a crime and you withhold information concerning him, you will be treated as an accessory to that crime?"

I was sure I saw a flicker of fear in Marie's eyes, but she stared back at the inspector coolly enough.

"I tell you, he has committed no crime."

The inspector shrugged. "Let us hope, for your sake, that you are right."

He stood up and paced back and forth for a few moments in the tiny room. When he sat down again, his face had softened and his dark eyes looked at the girl with fatherly concern.

"Now, Marie," he said, using her name for the first time, "let me put to you a hypothetical situation. A young man in Paris, a friend of yours, tells you that he may be the son of a very wealthy man. He hears that the man will be on a cruise in Burgundy this week. He knows that you have a holiday and he asks you to try to get acquainted with someone on the boat and find out whatever you can about the man.

"Accordingly, you strike up an acquaintance with the good-looking young captain. Then you have the unexpected good luck of being taken on as stewardess. However, even if this had not happened, you would still have been able to learn a good deal about the party on board through your acquaintance with the captain.

"You hear all the talk about Monsieur O'Connor and the making of his will, and you report this to your friend, who is hovering about in the vicinity. You describe to him where the Poppa's medicine is kept and that he must not have too much—"

"No! No! It is not true!"

The inspector did not pause. "Your friend slips onto the boat yesterday afternoon while everyone is out. He knows how to find the correct cabin from your description. He finds Monsieur O'Connor asleep. He opens the medicine bottle and drops several tablets into the wineglass, refilling it from the decanter.

"Then you meet him again that afternoon. Let us suppose that you do not know about his visit to the boat—that you believe, with the others, that the overdose was an accident. Now you tell your friend what has happened and that Monsieur O'Connor is in the hospital, probably dying. He says, what a terrible accident, but he is laughing to himself. He cautions you again not to reveal his identity. He knows that if trouble arises, he can claim that you were his accomplice."

Marie shuddered, and tears sprang from her eyes. "No! No! It is not possible! You are wrong!"

The inspector looked at her earnestly. "Then perhaps you had better tell us the truth."

Marie opened her mouth as if to speak, then shook her head. "I cannot tell you anything."

There was a long pause while the two stared at each other. Then the inspector shrugged. "You may go, Mademoiselle."

Marie gasped in surprise and ran quickly out of the room.

Andrew also looked surprised. "You let her go?"

Moreau grinned. "Oh, yes. She seems like a tough cookie, that little one, but you will see. Evidently she has not thought until now that her friend on the motorcycle could be guilty of this crime. Once she has time to think it over, she will not risk her own safety to cover up for him if she finds out that he is the killer!"

18

When Marie had left the police station, Inspector Moreau stepped to the door of the interrogation room and sent a police officer to the *Jacqueline* to bring Rosanna Rossi to the station.

"She is still a beautiful woman, is she not?" Moreau said to us. "I recognized her at once this morning on the boat."

"By the way," Andrew said to his friend, "the young tenor, Tonio Riccardi, is Rosanna's current lover. They are quite open about it, so I am hardly giving away state secrets."

Moreau began a new series of circles and squares on his notepad.

"I have been thinking about the episode of the Poppa's fall into the canal. Should we not now consider the possibility that this was an attempt on his life which did not succeed, and thus the killer tried again with the extra tablets of his medicine?"

"Yes, I've wondered about that ever since Ellen—Mrs. Walker—mentioned it earlier. I had forgotten it altogether because everyone felt at the time that poor Poppa was merely dramatizing.

A few minutes later Rosanna Rossi was shown into the little room, managing to make a regal entrance—the queen visiting her vassals, I thought with amusement.

The day had turned warm, and Rosanna wore a dark cotton dress with a deep V neck and a long strand of pearls. Her black hair was pulled back in a soft bun, and with her creamy skin and enormous dark eyes, she was strikingly attractive. She might pass for a good-looking forty, I thought, but she'll never look thirty again.

"Thank you for coming, Madame." Moreau looked at her almost reverently. "May I say that it has been my privilege and pleasure to hear you in the opera house on several occasions, each one a magnificent joy and a treasured memory?"

"Thank you, Inspector." She must hear this constantly, I thought. I wonder if anyone ever tires of adulation. Probably not, human nature being what it is.

"I have only a few questions for you," the inspector went on. "First, can you explain to me the nature of your disagreement with Monsieur O'Connor about a role at Glyndebourne of which I have been told?"

"Yes, of course. My friend Tonio Riccardi, the tenor, has been asked to sing Rodolfo next season at Glyndebourne. I wanted to sing Mimi opposite him, and since we are both under contract to O'Connor Enterprises, Poppa could easily have refused to sign Tonio unless they signed me as well."

"But if they refused, would this not deprive Monsieur Tonio of the role?"

"Oh, I'm sure they would have agreed in the end."

"Why did Monsieur O'Connor refuse your request?"

"In my opinion it was pure stubbornness. Poppa really had a thing about doing anything he was asked to do."

"Now that Mr. O'Connor is gone, who will make the decision about the opera contract?"

Rosanna looked at the inspector shrewdly. "It's up to Don Hubbard now. I think he will see it my way. I'll wait till things settle down and then talk to him about it."

"I see. Now, can you tell me about the Monday evening, when Monsieur O'Connor proclaimed that he was pushed into the canal? Where were you at the time of the—er—accident?"

"I was standing on the towpath near the place where the men were working on the lock. Tonio had gone to the boat to get my sweater, and I was waiting for him to come back when I heard a commotion, and the next thing I knew they were fishing Poppa out of the water. He must have been terrified, poor old dear. He had never learned to swim, you know."

"You have known Monsieur O'Connor for many years? Can you tell me about your relationship with him?"

"Of course. He really worked hard to get me started. You know, unless you have an agent who pushes you, it's hard to get anywhere in this business, no matter how good you are."

I noticed that Rosanna's regal manner was forgotten as she began to talk about her career.

"You see, I grew up in New York City, and in those days especially, it was very hard for American singers to get a foothold in our own country. The Metropolitan wanted the big names from abroad, and American singers had better luck in Europe. My name is Italian—my parents were second generation from Italy—but it still took me years to sing at the Met. Poppa had always been behind me through thick and thin—that's why I was so angry with him over Glyndebourne.''

"Angry enough to push him into the canal, perhaps merely as a prank?''

Rosanna's laugh gurgled up. ''No, Inspector, I didn't do that!''

Moreau turned another page in his notebook, glancing at Dupuis to see that the taping was in progress.

"Now, Madame, purely as a routine, will you describe to me your movements yesterday afternoon from the end of the luncheon until Monsieur O'Connor was taken to the hospital?''

"Let's see. After lunch we were on our own to walk around here in Tournus. I decided to wear pants and a sweater and comfortable shoes. Tonio came in to wait for me while I dressed. He is my—er—companion, you understand?''

She looked at the inspector as if to say, You are a man of the world, I need not explain.

The inspector's French soul responded promptly. ''But of course, Madame!''

"By the time we went up on deck everyone else had apparently gone, so we walked up the hill to the Abbey and went all through it—up the circular stairs to the chapel above, down into the crypt, the whole bit. What a marvelous place it is!''

"Did you see other members of your party at this time?''

"Oh, yes. We passed each other here and there. I believe you were there, Andrew?''

"Yes, I'm sure I saw you somewhere, but I can't say exactly where.''

"Anyhow, after that a few of us met at a little café across from the Abbey.'' She turned to Andrew. ''You and Don and the little girl pianist—Julie—were sitting outdoors at a table and Tonio and I sat down with you.''

"Yes," Andrew said. "Jane, you and Molly and Ellen were still in the Abbey, I believe.''

I nodded.

Rosanna went on. "I didn't stay long. Tonio was being stupid and I just walked off.''

"Can you explain, Madame? What was the behavior of Monsieur Tonio?''

"Well, Tonio started flirting with the girl Julie, telling her how beautiful she was and what a wonderful pianist and so on. I could see that Don Hubbard didn't like it at all. I think he's crazy about her, but he obviously had no right to object. At any rate, I had had enough, so I left.''

"And where did you go, Madame?''

"I looked in some of the little shops and then turned up the hill and found that tiny park—sort of a triangle, enclosed in railings. I wandered inside and sat down on a bench among the trees and shrubbery. I must have sat there for quite a while, just thinking. Then I walked on around the outside of the Abbey and followed some little streets until I came down to the river and walked along back to the boat.''

"About what time was it when you returned to the *Jacqueline?*''

"I don't know. It must have been about half past three, I suppose.''

"And then, Madame?''

"Oh, Tonio was there. He said he had looked everywhere for me. He apologized for flirting with the girl and—well, in short, we made up. Then he went and got the cards and we played gin rummy until we heard Molly calling out that something was wrong with Poppa.''

"Where did you sit to play your cards?"

"At a table in the salon."

"During the time you played the cards, can you remember who came or went?"

"Only Karl and Julie. The car came for them just a few minutes before Molly came back, and they came up the stairs carrying their suitcases. I believe they were planning to change in Lyon before the recital."

"Did you see any members of the crew during this time?"

"No. I don't remember seeing anyone else until Molly came back alone and went downstairs and found Poppa unconscious. It was after the ambulance had gone that Stephen Shaw and the captain and Marie all came on board. We told them what had happened. Then"—to Andrew and me—"the rest of you arrived and we told all of you about Poppa."

The inspector cleared his throat. "Thank you, Madame. Just one more question. Will you describe to me what you remember of the circumstances at the Abbey last evening when Madame O'Connor was attacked?"

Rosanna recounted the events of the evening as Ellen had described them earlier—how we went in to listen to the service, how we were surprised not to find Molly when we were ready to leave, how everyone searched, and how they heard me call out for help as I came up from the crypt.

"I believe that will be all, Madame. Thank you again for your cooperation."

As she rose to leave, Rosanna looked at the inspector shrewdly and said, "I didn't kill Poppa—and what's more, I don't have any idea who did."

When she had gone, Moreau looked at us in surprise. "What did she mean by that? That is the one question I would never have thought to ask her!"

*   *   *

After the interview with Rosanna, the inspector noted that it was approaching one o'clock. "You two may as well go back to the boat for your luncheon. The sergeant and I will get something here in the town."

Consulting the lists in front of him, the inspector added, "This afternoon I believe we shall see the young lady—Mademoiselle Bergstrom—and then the two gentleman guests. Finally, we shall speak to the remaining members of the crew. Perhaps you can bring the young lady with you when you return?"

The luncheon on board was another gloomy affair. Ellen reported that Molly was more exhausted than she had realized and arranged for Marie to take a tray to her in Ellen's and my cabin, since Molly's own cabin was sealed by the police.

Everyone had been asked to remain available for questioning, and although the common assumption was that the questions were routine, there was nevertheless an atmosphere of discomfort added to the double shock of Poppa's death and the attack on Molly.

Andrew and I were naturally regarded as the source of inside information and were asked about the police view of the case. I left it to Andrew to answer vaguely, and he merely reported the order in which the inspector wanted to interview the rest of the people on board.

Stephen Shaw managed to take me aside at the end of lunch. His shirt was buttoned nearly to his neck today, I noticed, a concession to the seriousness of the situation, no doubt.

"My dear Jane, all this is most distressing. I've been in touch with the people at the Paris office, of course, and they're offering me no help at all. I'm just to carry on and try to keep everyone happy! Rather a tall order, wouldn't you say?"

"But, Stephen, I don't see really what anyone can do. We simply have to wait till the police sort it out, don't you think?"

"Yes, I suppose you're right. You're such a comfort, Jane. Who would ever have guessed that anything so dreadful could happen on one of our cruises?"

After a few more soothing phrases I went to join Andrew and Julie, who were ready to leave for the police station.

When we had left the boat, Julie looked at each of us in turn, her beautiful eyes troubled.

"Jane, Andrew, I want to ask your advice. You remember what I told you the other day about hating Mr. O'Connor because of what he did to my brother? Well, do you think I should tell the police about it? After all, they do want to know if anyone had a grudge against him, I suppose?"

Andrew considered. "I don't know, Julie. Jane and I would certainly not betray your confidence unless we believed it was pertinent to the investigation, and I find it hard to believe that you had anything to do with Poppa O'Connor's death." He looked at me for confirmation, and I nodded.

Julie said, "No, of course I had nothing to do with it. But if the inspector heard about it from someone else, then he would think I was hiding something, wouldn't he?"

I said, "Yes, I suppose he might."

"I've talked to Don about it." When she mentioned Don's name, Julie's usually serious face lighted up with an inner glow which made me think maybe there was some hope for Don in his obvious infatuation for the girl.

"I told him the whole story," Julie went on, "and

he was wonderful about it. He said that Poppa had made lots of enemies through the years, although he was sure that he had never really meant to harm anyone. He said it was just Poppa's way."

I asked, "Did Don think you should tell the police about your feelings toward his stepfather?"

"He didn't know. He said to ask you two about it."

Andrew thought for a moment. "How do you feel yourself about telling the inspector your story?"

"Oh, I wouldn't mind at all if I thought he would understand. Since he is a friend of yours, we thought you would know best."

"Yes, I've known Bernard for some years, and I believe that he's completely fair and honest in his dealings. If he believes you are innocent, your story would have no effect, but if he believed you were in any way involved in a crime, he would be implacable."

Julie merely said, "I see. Thank you."

At the police station Julie was asked to wait while we went in to join the inspector.

"I have some disturbing news for you," Moreau began. "I sent to my office in Lyon for one of my own technicians, and here is his preliminary report on the objects taken from the cabin of Monsieur O'Connor and the candlestick found beside Madame O'Connor after she was attacked. The candlestick had been wiped clean of fingerprints but shows blood and hair where the scalp was lacerated. As for the wineglass, there are traces of the medicine inside the glass, so someone must have dropped some tablets of the medicine into the glass, is it not so?"

Andrew considered, "If it is a mere trace, I suppose Poppa might have only partially swallowed the last tablet taken and therefore have left a small amount of medicine clinging to the glass."

"Yes, but unfortunately my expert believes that the

amount of medicine coating the bottom of the glass is not consistent with that theory. It is not likely that the Poppa himself would drop his tablets into the wine-glass before taking them. However, if someone else had dropped some tablets into his wine, would he not have noticed the taste and stopped before swallowing the remainder of the glass?''

I spoke up. ''Probably not. Poppa always tossed off his wine rapidly, and he was one of those people whose taste buds are quite blunt. In fact, he was rather boastful about it.''

''I see. Now, as for the fingerprints, what we have learned may be significant. The technician has found only two sets of prints on the decanter and the wine-glass on Monsieur O'Connor's bedside table. The medicine bottle is plastic and therefore does not produce much in the way of fingerprints, but the fragments he has appear to be the same as those on the glass objects. One set are those of the Poppa, and we have to assume that the others belong to his wife. I have sent a man to the boat to obtain a set of her prints and we should soon have the report.''

Andrew frowned. ''The objects had not been wiped off, then?''

''No, but of course anyone wishing to disguise his fingerprints could easily have used a handkerchief when handling the objects on the table.''

''I noticed a box of tissues on the shelf. Would a tissue work as well?''

''Yes, certainly. A good point, since not many people go about carrying handkerchiefs these days. Besides, *mon ami,* if someone wished to preserve the appearance that the overdose was an accident, he would not wish to wipe off the prints of the Poppa and Momma.''

''Yes, of course.''

The inspector drew a square on his notepad and placed a circle inside it. "I have been thinking. Either the medicine was placed in the glass while Monsieur O'Connor was still awake—that is, soon after his wife left the cabin at shortly after two o'clock—or it was done later on, presumably after he had gone to sleep, in which case we presume that the first glass of wine had been taken and the person poured additional wine into the glass from the decanter. Would it have been possible for anyone, in the first instance, to add tablets to his glass while he was still awake?"

I answered again. "Oddly enough, I think it might. Poppa was not at all observant of his surroundings. If his attention was distracted even briefly, I believe someone could have dropped some tablets into the wineglass which Molly had filled before leaving. However, the person certainly could not have poured wine from the decanter—even Poppa would have noticed that! But if we presume a time soon after two o'clock, he would not yet have drunk the wine in the glass."

"This would have to be a person familiar enough to enter his cabin while he was preparing to sleep. Would that not exclude many of those on board?"

"No, not if you knew Poppa. He was quite uninhibited. Anyone, even a member of the crew, could have come into his cabin on some pretext while he was sitting up in bed and Poppa wouldn't have been in the least embarrassed."

"I see. Of course, if the tablets were placed in the glass after he had gone to sleep, when would he have taken the fatal glass of wine?"

Andrew frowned. "Don Hubbard mentioned that Poppa might doze off, then wake up and take his second glass. However, it wouldn't have to be that way at all. Suppose that after Molly leaves and he has finished his phone call, Poppa takes his two tablets as usual and drops off to sleep. Then the killer slips in, drops extra tablets into the glass, and refills it from the decanter. If Poppa should awaken and see him there, he has only to smile and say he came to make sure Poppa was resting comfortably.

"Now, Poppa wakes up sometime before Molly returns at half past four, and decides to drink the extra glass of wine—not to get to sleep but simply because he likes wine and hasn't had his second glass.

"Remember, we have no way of knowing what time Poppa woke up—only that he was in a coma when Molly returned. According to the doctor, there is no way to tell what time he took the overdose. It might have been soon after two o'clock, or it might have been after four o'clock. The only one who knows the answer to that is the person who murdered Poppa!"

19

When Julie Bergstrom was shown into the room and had taken her seat, I noticed that Inspector Moreau took in the girl's beauty, although his manner remained impassive.

"I have some very serious news to impart to you, Mademoiselle Bergstrom. A short time ago we acquired evidence which indicates that Monsieur O'Connor's death was not the result of an accident but was probably perpetrated by someone who intended to kill him."

Julie gasped. "How awful! Surely it must be a mistake?"

"No, Mademoiselle, it is no mistake. You are the first to be told of this, but I intend for everyone concerned to know at once. I have sent a police officer to the *Jacqueline* to inform all of the guests and members of the crew and to make certain that no one leaves the premises."

Since everyone had already been instructed to await interviews with the police, the inspector had told us he now intended to put some pressure on. The announcement would not alert the killer, for presumably he or she would already have a story ready for the police, but the others might be more forthcoming if they were aware of the seriousness of the case.

"Now, Mademoiselle," the inspector was saying to Julie, "will you tell me please how you came to be on the boat this week?"

Julie explained about the two recitals with Karl Gebler and that it was he who had been invited on the cruise. "Karl insisted that I come along."

"You were not previously acquainted with Monsieur O'Connor?"

Julie glanced at us. "No, I had not met him personally. But there is something I want to tell you about." And she launched into the story of her brother's unhappy experience with Poppa, adding some details that she had not told us in our conversation that day in the garden of the château.

"You see, Eric was very proud, but when his bookings began to fall off, he went to Mr. O'Connor and told him how desperately he felt about his career— that it was his whole life. He begged him to help, but Mr. O'Connor just waved him away and said he couldn't do anything for him. He had assigned Eric to a member of his staff who was inexperienced, and that's why Eric went to Mr. O'Connor himself to plead his case."

Julie's face flushed with anger as she relived her brother's humiliation. "Then Eric said he would break his contract with O'Connor Enterprises, and Mr. O'Connor flew into a rage and told him that good violinists were a dime a dozen and he'd better not try anything like that or he would see that he never played in public again! It was awful—poor Eric."

"Was Mr. Don Hubbard a member of the agency at that time?"

"Oh, no. This was more than ten years ago. I was only a child at the time, and Don would have been at college."

Stopping to draw a deep breath, Julie went on. "You see, Inspector, I had good reason to dislike Mr. O'Connor, but I want you to know that I had nothing to do with his death."

"Thank you, Mademoiselle. Now, can you tell me your whereabouts on Monday evening, at the time Monsieur O'Connor fell into the canal?"

Julie looked surprised. "Oh, let's see. Five of us took out the bicycles." She smiled at Andrew and me. "We rode past the lock and a long way down the towpath. Then we stopped to sit on some logs and talk for a while. As we started back, we saw a lane leading off into the fields and Don said, 'Come on!' but I must have been the only one who heard him because I followed and pretty soon I looked around and the others were not there."

"And how long was it before you returned to the area of the lock?"

"I don't have any idea. We found an old deserted farmhouse and tried to look inside, but it was boarded up. Then we rode back to the canal and sat talking for a while. Suddenly we realized it was quite dark."

Julie flushed slightly, then went on. "When we got back near the lock, Don left his bike and went ahead to see how the work was coming. There were people milling around and pretty soon I heard shouts and splashings in the water. I ran up to see what happened and heard that Mr. O'Connor had fallen into the canal."

"You could not see who was standing near him at the time?"

"No. I didn't even know he was there!"

The inspector rose and paced back and forth in the little room, then sat down again.

"I understand, Mademoiselle, that you and Monsieur Gebler were in Lyon on Wednesday evening giving a recital. Thus you were not present at the time of the attack on Madame O'Connor. However, can you tell me where you were after luncheon on that day and at what time you departed for Lyon?"

Julie described our bike ride up the hill with Molly, and how everyone had toured the Abbey.

"Then some of us were sitting outside at a café in the square when Rosanna and Tonio came to sit with us."

Julie paused uncertainly.

"And then?" prompted the inspector.

"Well, I'm afraid Rosanna was angry because Tonio was—well, paying me some compliments. Anyhow, she walked off. After a while Don and I went into some of the little shops and bought some souvenirs." She smiled shyly. "Then I realized it was almost four o'clock and the car was coming for Karl and me at a quarter after four. I took my bike and rode off down the hill. Don said he would wait for his mother and sister. When I got to the boat, Karl was standing on the deck and we went down to our cabins. We had already packed our bags, and when we came back up, the car was there. We took the driver back to his garage and drove on to Lyon."

"Thank you, Mademoiselle, that will be all."

When Julie had gone, Moreau looked at Andrew and his eyes twinkled.

"*Eh bien,* I should say that Monsieur 'Don' is a fortunate young man, is it not so?"

*   *   *

"And now for our two young gentlemen," said Moreau. "The tenor and then the violinist. In a moment we shall hear what they have to say for themselves. But first, what can you tell me about the Poppa's former wife, Madame Odette. Is she a reliable person, so far as you know?"

"I should say quite the contrary," Andrew repeated what Poppa had told us of Odette. "The very fact that she was playing games with Poppa and being secretive about the whole situation makes one wonder what she was up to."

"Her husband here in France died two years or so ago?"

"Yes, so she told Poppa."

"Very well, we shall see."

When Tonio Riccardi came in and was seated, he looked at the inspector with dark, serious eyes. "It is true that Signor O'Connor did not die of the accident?"

"Yes, we believe that is true."

"Then what is it that happened? The officer did not tell us."

The inspector smiled slightly. "No, he was instructed not to tell you."

"Oh, but of course. I understand. How can I help you, Inspector?"

"You may tell us first your movements of yesterday afternoon after luncheon."

"Yes. I believe Signora Rossi has already told you—?"

"We have her report, yes. Perhaps you will tell us in your own words?"

"Of course." Tonio described waiting for Rosanna to change and noting that when they left the boat, everyone else seemed to have gone.

"Then we made a visit to the Abbey and afterward

sat at a table in the square. I am afraid I behaved rather foolishly. I paid compliments to the lovely Miss Julie and the Signora became angry with me and walked away." A little complacent smile appeared on Tonio's handsome face.

"And then, Monsieur?"

"Then the Signorina went off with Don Hubbard." Tonio looked at Andrew. "You and I sat talking for a few minutes, did we not?"

"Yes, that is correct."

"Then the others came along. After a little while I excused myself and went to look for Signora Rosanna, but I could not find her, so I went back to the boat. I looked in her cabin, but she was not there, so I went up on deck to wait for her."

"About what time was this?"

"I can tell you precisely, because I was looking at my watch as I waited. It was a quarter past three when I returned to the deck and half past three when the Signora returned. Then I begged her pardon for my behavior and we played gin rummy in the salon."

"You were able to see the top of the stairs from where you sat?"

"Yes, indeed. As the Signora has told you, we saw no one until the violinist and Miss Julie came to get their bags. Then Signora O'Connor returned and cried out for help and I used the telephone in the salon to call the ambulance."

"Thank you. Now, Monsieur Riccardi, I should like to know if your parents are living and, if so, what is their address?"

Tonio looked startled. "My parents?"

"Yes, please."

Tonio's voice was distressed. "My parents are living apart. It is very sad, but these things happen. My father lives in Rome and my mother in San Remo, where her family resides." Referring to a small address book, he read out two addresses.

The inspector continued. "San Remo is, of course, on the Riviera. Does your mother sometimes come to Paris?"

"Not often, no."

"And when did you last see your mother?"

Tonio hesitated. "It was two months ago, in April. I sent for her to come to London, where I was singing Alfredo in *Traviata* at Covent Garden. The journey was expensive, but it meant a great deal to her. She is very proud of my success."

I reflected that to the layman this might sound boastful, but in fact performers talk about their careers as frankly as businessmen do about theirs. Like a young executive who has received a big promotion in his corporation, Tonio's leading role at the Royal Opera House was a major step in his climb to the top.

Meanwhile the inspector was saying, "You paid for your mother's visit to London, then. Does your father not provide for your mother?"

Tonio's face flushed darkly. "Not as much as he ought to."

"Then extra money would be welcome to your mother?"

Tonio gave no sign of comprehension. He looked at the inspector with round, innocent eyes. "But of course. Is this not true for everyone?"

Moreau then took Tonio through the events of the evening when Poppa fell into the canal, and Tonio confirmed Rosanna's account, declaring that he was just returning from the boat with her sweater when he heard the commotion and saw Poppa being plucked from the water.

He showed no further sign of discomfort until the

inspector questioned him about the visit to the Abbey the evening before.

"When the service ended," Moreau went on, "what did you do next?"

Tonio's eyes shifted for the first time, and he looked at the wall, then down at the table. "I excused myself to Signora Rosanna and went into the side chapel, where there are candles."

"The Signora did not come with you?"

"No. She no longer practices the faith. I believe she guessed what I wanted to do and went to join the others. I put in my offering, lit a candle, and knelt in prayer for a time."

"You said that you had visited the Abbey earlier that day. Was the chapel in which you knelt near the steps leading down to the crypt?"

Again the look of innocence. "Yes, I believe it was."

"Now, Signor Riccardi, I believe that you were aware, along with others on the boat, that Madame O'Connor wanted her husband to make a will and that he finally consented and did so. Can you tell me what you believe to be the provisions of the will, generally speaking?"

"I believe he divided his fortune among what might be called his three children—that is, the son by his first wife, and his stepchildren, Don Hubbard and Ellen Walker."

"Thank you. One final question, Monsieur Riccardi. What is your age?"

"My age? I am twenty-five."

"And your birthday?"

"The third of June—this month."

When Tonio had been excused, Moreau looked at Andrew. "So, what do you think? An excellent actor—or—?"

Andrew smiled. "Remember, for the opera he needs to be a good actor as well as a good singer!"

With a Gallic shrug Moreau looked at his list. "Monsieur Gebler should be here by now. The last of the guests." He nodded to the sergeant, and Karl Gebler came in and took his seat at the table.

The questioning of Karl followed much the same pattern as that of Tonio. The inspector began with Karl's movements of the afternoon before and then moved to the evening of Poppa's fall into the canal. What emerged from his answers was that Karl was a good deal of a loner. He had remained in his cabin the afternoon before, working on his violin.

"I changed the D string. It gave me some trouble during rehearsal. Then I rubbed the wood. I wanted everything in readiness for the evening recital, you understand? I heard the singer and her boyfriend talking as they came along the passage. Then all was quiet for a time. When I had finished with the violin, I decided to go for a walk in the town."

"Had the others left the boat by that time?"

"I presumed they had gone, but then I thought I heard a door closing, so I cannot be sure."

"At what time was this?"

"I don't know. I suppose between half past two and a quarter to three. Something like that."

"Was the sound at your end of the passage, that is, near Monsieur O'Connor's cabin?"

Karl paused. "No. If anything, I should have thought it was at the other end. But then, I am not sure that I heard anything at all."

Karl then described how he had walked up to the Abbey, going around the far side to see the exterior before entering the church at the west door. Thus he had not encountered the others in the party, who by this time were seated at the café or were wandering through the shops on the nearer side of the Abbey.

When he left the Abbey, Karl described walking up the hill and stopping for a coffee. Then he continued his walk, coming down to the river and walking along the road toward where the boat was moored.

"At a café near the bridge I saw Stephen Shaw, our guide, sitting at a table outside and joined him for an aperitif. We talked for a time and then I saw that it was after four o'clock and I had to go to be ready for the car. Just as I reached the boat Julie came along with her bicycle and we went down to get our bags."

As for the night of the incident on the canal, Karl reported that he saw Poppa start out for his walk along the towpath leading away from the damaged lock and that he himself had left the boat and walked in the direction of the lock, continuing on for some distance along the path.

"Did you see any members of your party at this time?"

"I might have. I didn't particularly notice. There were also many other people about, coming and going. Some chap on a motorbike went by and nearly knocked me over. That's all I remember."

He had turned back toward the lock, Karl went on, and stood watching the men at work. Before the lock was fixed, he heard a cry and a splash but had no idea who it was until Poppa was brought out of the water.

"Everyone was making a great to-do," he added with his disdainful air, "so I stayed away."

"Now, Monsieur Gebler, where was your place of birth?"

"I was born in Heidelberg."

"Your parents are both German?"

"No, my mother is French."

"And where do your parents now reside?"

"My father is dead. My mother lives in Strasbourg."

"Does your mother often go to Paris?"

"Yes. My aunt—her sister—lives in Paris."

"How long ago did your father's death occur?"

"It is three years now."

"What was his occupation?"

"He was the owner of a textile company."

"A prosperous company?"

"Yes."

The inspector paused, and Andrew indicated that he wanted to ask a question.

"When we were in Paris last Saturday evening, you may remember that Jane and I came to your recital. Instead of returning to the hotel with us in the taxi, you said you preferred to walk. Yet as we went out the stage door, Jane saw you step into a taxi. Can you tell us why the little deception and where you were in fact going?"

For the first time, Karl's face flushed in anger and he glared at me. "That is purely a personal matter. I do not wish to discuss it."

Andrew's expression remained impassive. "Thank you," he said, nodding to the inspector.

"Monsieur Gebler, you were aware, of course, of the discussion about Monsieur O'Connor's will and that he did in fact make a will. What do you understand were the provisions of that will?"

"Everyone was saying that he left his property to a son by his first wife and to his stepchildren, in equal parts."

"What was your opinion of Monsieur O'Connor?"

"He was a wonderful man!"

"Do you know whether he had any enemies?"

A little gleam of malice appeared in Gebler's eyes. "I know someone who hated him—my pianist, Julie!"

"Yes, she has told us about that."

Karl's mouth opened in astonishment. "She told you herself?"

"Yes. Some people are quite open and hold nothing back from the police."

The inspector's irony was lost on Karl, who merely looked disappointed that his bombshell had proved a dud.

"One last question, Monsieur Gebler. What is your age?"

"I am twenty-four."

"And when is your birthday?"

"One month from now, the twentieth of July."

20

When Karl Gebler had been excused, Inspector Moreau suggested we take a short break. Over coffee and rolls we talked about the possibilities suggested by the evidence gathered so far but came to no useful conclusions.

Presently the inspector said, *"Eh, bien,* and now for the gentlemen of the crew."

Stephen Shaw was shown in and took his seat, trying to appear elegantly at ease but managing only to resemble a worried schoolmaster, despite his blond good looks.

"This is all quite dreadful, Inspector," Stephen began, twisting the gold chain that hung over his shirt. "We at Euro-Cruises like to provide an atmosphere of peace and relaxation for our patrons—"

The inspector caressed his mustache, half hiding a wry smile. "Yes, I understand, Monsieur Shaw. But if the crimes occur, we must investigate, is it not so? Now, Monsieur, will you please tell me what is your age?"

"I am twenty-five, sir."

"And your parents, they are living?"

"Yes. They are at present traveling in New Zealand."

"And the nationality of your parents?"

Stephen looked surprised. "They are both English."

"And on Monday evening, when Monsieur O'Connor—er—fell into the canal, where were you at the time?"

Stephen said he had crossed the little bridge formed by the arms of the lock and was on the other side of the canal when he heard a cry, followed by a splash, and saw the lockkeeper's son kick off his shoes and dive into the water. He had no idea who had fallen in until afterward.

"And now will you please describe your movements yesterday afternoon?"

"Yes, of course. After luncheon I took a long walk along the river. With the larger tours I usually remain available to my people in case they want me to accompany them to the Abbey or about the town. With this group I felt that my services were not required. They are all self-sufficient and experienced travelers."

"And after your walk?"

"I sat in the café on the quay. Karl Gebler, the violinist, came along and we chatted for a bit. Then it was time for him to go to Lyon. I saw the car come for him and Miss Bergstrom. Later on, Marie and Emile came to join me and the three of us went along to a café where there's a dart board. We played darts for a while, then walked back to the boat."

"At what time did you return to the boat?"

"It must have been about five o'clock when we went aboard. It was then that we heard the shocking news about Mr. O'Connor from Madame Rossi and Signor

Riccardi. The other guests arrived soon afterward."

As for the time of the attack on Molly the evening before, Stephen stated that as he had told Andrew when they met outside the Abbey, he had been on his way to the hospital to inquire about Poppa when he heard the music of the service and stepped inside to listen. When Andrew told him that there was no change in Poppa's condition, he had gone back down the hill toward the boat.

"You no doubt heard the talk about Monsieur O'Connor's will. Do you know how it was resolved?"

"I understood that he had made a will providing equally for his stepchildren and his own son."

"Have you anything further to add, Monsieur?"

"No, I'm afraid not."

"Then that will be all for now. Thank you, Monsieur."

When Stephen had been excused and Philippe had entered and folded his long, slender body into the chair, the inspector began with a compliment. "I have been told of your excellent cuisine. I regret that under the circumstances I do not have the opportunity to partake of your artistry."

The two spoke of food and cooking with the absorption that only Frenchmen could share. At last the inspector paused regretfully.

"We must now speak of other matters, *n'est-ce pas?* What did you do yesterday afternoon when the luncheon was over?"

Philippe considered. "By two o'clock everyone had finished. Marie helped me clean up. Then she went out to our deck and sat at the table with the captain. I saw that they were looking at a large sheet of yellow paper, but when I came to sit down, the captain quickly folded it up and put it into the pocket of his shirt. They are so silly, those two. What do I care for their secrets?"

"Are they on intimate terms?"

Philippe shrugged. "But of course. He spends the night in her cabin."

"And after luncheon, where did you go?"

"I went to lie on my bunk and listen to my tapes. I have a collection of the best rock groups."

"You listen with earphones?"

"Yes. We are not permitted to have the stereos. They would disturb the guests."

Thank heaven for that, I thought, exchanging a smile with Andrew.

"So you were not able to hear anything which might have taken place on the boat at that time?"

"No, Monsieur."

"Did you leave the boat at any time in the afternoon?"

"Yes. About three o'clock I went into the town to buy a pack of cigarettes. I was gone only ten minutes."

"Were the captain and Marie still aboard at that time?"

"No, I didn't see them."

"When you are in your bunk you cannot see the gangplank or the entrance to the salon?"

"No, Monsieur."

"And you heard nothing?"

"No, nothing. That is, except the singing."

The inspector sat up sharply. "The singing?"

"Yes. Once when I took off the headset and reached under my bunk for a box of tapes, that was when I heard the opera singer."

"Monsieur Riccardi, the tenor?"

"No, no, the lady."

"Was she at the piano?"

Philippe shook his head. "No, the piano is very loud, even in the crew's quarters. I did not hear the piano. Besides, the sound was coming up from below."

"Madame Rossi's cabin is almost directly below your quarters, is it not? Did the sound appear to come from there?"

"Yes, as nearly as I could tell."

"At what time was this?"

"Perhaps a quarter to three. I cannot be sure."

"How long did the singing continue?"

"Oh, that I don't know. I put my tape in, and of course after that I could no longer hear."

"Could it have been after three o'clock when you heard the lady singing?"

"No, it was before I went to get the cigarettes, and I know that was at three o'clock because I looked at the clock and I remember thinking that I still have some time before I must begin my preparations for dinner."

Further questioning produced no addition to Philippe's story. He stated that he knew nothing concerning Poppa's fall into the canal, and as for the attack on Molly at the Abbey the evening before, he had not gone up into the town until after nine o'clock. He had no idea about the provisions of Poppa's will. The others were talking about it, but he had paid little attention.

Finally Philippe declared that he was twenty-six years of age and that his parents, both French, lived in Rouen. His birthday was the tenth of January.

After Philippe's departure the inspector stood up. "I shall ask to have Madame Rossi brought back in."

I said, "Excuse me, Inspector, but since an officer is going to the boat, may I make a request?"

159

"But of course."

I described certain items I had seen in the cabin occupied by Poppa and Molly and explained why I thought they might be helpful to the investigation. The inspector nodded and requested that the officer sent to fetch Rosanna also open the O'Connors' cabin and bring the items back to the station.

Back in the interrogation room, Moreau looked at us with raised brows.

"So what have we now? If Madame Rosanna did come back to the boat instead of sitting in the park as she told us, would she have been there before three o'clock, when Philippe heard the singing?"

Andrew considered. "Yes, it would have been some time after two-thirty that Tonio went into his act with Julie, and Rosanna stalked off. The boat is only minutes away."

"So if she went back to the boat, why does she lie about it?"

"Yes. And even more baffling—if she actually came back to drop medicine into Poppa's glass, why sing at the top of her voice to advertise that she was there?"

"Exactly. Of course, she probably assumed everyone was gone."

Andrew took another sip of his coffee. "There is one possibility, although it seems unlikely. Sometimes singers run practice scales and roulades so automatically they're unaware they are doing it, just as you or I might mutter aloud to ourselves when we are thinking about something."

"I see. She might have begun without thinking and then stopped abruptly, realizing what she had done. Philippe heard only a fragment, we may suppose, before returning to his frightful tapes. So we shall now hear what Madame has to say."

But a second interview with Rosanna produced no

further light. She flatly denied having returned to the boat before three-thirty, insisting that she had done exactly what she had told the inspector earlier. She seemed to be neither indignant nor frightened. In fact, there was a glint of amusement in her expression which seemed to say, Well, well, the great detectives are baffled. Let them work it out!

"So, only one left on our list—the captain."

As the inspector spoke, an officer entered and handed him a sheet of paper. Moreau took it and pushed some other pages to one side, so that by chance I could see what was written on the top sheet.

"Here is the report on the fingerprints," the inspector was saying. "As we thought, the only other set on the objects from the Poppa's cabin are those of his wife."

But I was scarcely listening, for on the sheet lying before me was the official list of the crew members which Stephen Shaw had given to the inspector that morning and which he had slipped under the list giving the names of the guests. Now I saw something that caught my eye:

GUIDE	Stephen Edward Shaw
CAPTAIN	Emile Michel Arnaud
CHEF	Philippe Albert Berger
STEWARDESS	Francine Mathilde Gilbert

The last name had been crossed out and "Marie Dupont" written beside it.

"Look at this!" I said. Andrew and the inspector, examining the list, saw what I meant.

"So, my friends," exclaimed the inspector, "is it possible we have the answer to our problem?"

21

Emile came into the interrogation room at the police station with a swagger, stretched his long legs under the table, and pulled out a pack of cigarettes.

"All right if I smoke?"

Inspector Moreau gave him an icy stare. "No, it is *not* all right."

Emile shrugged and put the cigarettes back into the pocket of his jeans.

"Your full name?"

"Emile Michel Arnaud."

"Your place of birth?"

"Marseille."

"Your age?"

"I was twenty-five one week ago."

"Have you ever been known by your middle name, Michel?"

Emile frowned. "No. Why do you ask?"

Without replying, the inspector went on.

"Your present address?"

"I have no address. I live on the boat for eight months of the year."

"And the other four?"

"I take off and travel, or just bum around. Not a bad life, eh?"

"At what address do you receive your mail in the off season?"

Emile frowned again. "I check in with the company office in Paris and let them know where I am. If there is anything important, they send it on."

I wondered if Emile was lying and if the inspector thought so, too, but Moreau simply shifted to another line of questioning.

"Will you please tell me exactly what you did yesterday afternoon after lunch?"

"Yesterday?"

"Yes. That was the day Monsieur O'Connor was taken to the hospital."

"Oh, shit, you don't think I had anything to do with that?"

"Just answer the question."

"Well, while Marie and Philippe were cleaning up, I checked the oil pressure and the generator. Then Marie came out on our deck and we talked for a while."

"What was on the sheet of yellow paper you were looking at with Marie?"

"Oh, so Philippe noticed that, did he? Well, it was just something of Marie's. It's not important."

"I'll be the judge of what is important."

"Okay, what do you want me to say? It was a secret map leading to the place where the fucking treasure is buried?"

The inspector looked at him levelly. "Arnaud, I strongly advise you not to be a smart-ass. If the paper belonged to Marie, why did you fold it and put it away in your shirt pocket?''

"Obviously I didn't want Philippe to see it."

"And where is the paper now?"

"It's gone out with the trash."

"Then perhaps you would like to tell us what was on the paper?"

Emile had clearly been playing for time and now came up with an answer. "It was a letter somebody had written to Marie. Some guy had been bothering her and she asked my advice about it."

This was so patently lame that the inspector merely raised an eyebrow and went on. "After you had—shall we say—advised Marie about her love life, what did you do next?"

"I said to Marie, 'Let's go into the town.' She said, 'Go ahead and I'll meet you up there.' So I did."

"At what time was this?"

"Oh, hell, how would I know?" Emile smirked. "Sorry *sir.*" Then with mock formality: "I did not specifically consult my timepiece at that moment, but I would hazard a conjecture that it was approximately three o'clock when Mademoiselle joined me at the café by the bridge."

Ignoring Emile's antics, the inspector moved smoothly on. "Did you see any of the guests on the boat, or entering or leaving the boat, at this time?"

Emile dropped his nonsense and thought for a moment. "No, I don't think so."

"Or did you hear anything, such as the sound of the piano, or singing, perhaps, as you were leaving the boat?"

Emile shook his head. "No, nothing like that."

"And how long was it before Marie appeared at the café?"

"I don't know. A few minutes."

"And then?"

"We looked in the shops for a while and then went into a bar for a drink. We walked along the river and on the way back we saw Shaw, and the three of us went to a place he likes, where they have a dart board. We played for a while and then went back to the boat—probably about five o'clock."

When questioned about his whereabouts on the evening when Poppa fell into the canal, Emile stated that he and Marie had crossed the bridge but had not gone far along the towpath. "I had to stick around because once the lock was fixed, I would have to get the boat through right away."

They both heard a splash and saw the boy pull off his shoes and dive into the water, but they did not know at the time who had fallen.

As for the attack on Molly, Emile admitted to being in the vicinity of the Abbey but denied having entered the church.

"I heard the singing but no way did I want to go in. Shit, I haven't gone to church since I was thirteen, and I'm not going to start now."

"Was Marie with you at this time?"

Emile scowled. "No. She had gone off somewhere."

"Now, Arnaud, you no doubt heard the talk on the *Jacqueline* about Monsieur O'Connor making a will. What do you understand were the provisions of his will?"

Emile looked straight into the inspector's eyes. "All I know is what everybody said—that everything would go to his wife and then after that to his three kids. That is, Mrs. Walker and Mr. Hubbard, and a son by a former wife."

"Is your father living, Arnaud?"

Emile laughed bitterly. "My father? No, he's dead, the bastard."

"And your mother?"

A hesitation. "Yes, she is living."

"In Paris?"

"Yes."

"What is her address, please?"

Suddenly Emile's face stiffened with anger.

"I'm not going to tell you. I don't give a damn what you do. It's none of your affair, and you can go to hell for all I care!"

The inspector ignored this outburst as he had ignored Emile's attempts at humor. "Is there anything further you can tell us that might shed any light on this investigation?"

Emile's answer was a snarl. "What in hell would I know about it? I don't have anything to do with these rich bastards and who is going to get their money. I only wish I did. But I'll tell you this. There's a guy on a motorcycle Marie has been meeting. Everywhere we go he is lurking around. You might try asking him some questions and leave me out of it!"

Moreau paused and studied his pad of notes. Then he sighed. "All right, Arnaud. You will be escorted back to the boat now. Please remain on board. Remember, a police officer is stationed at the foot of the gangplank."

Emile stood up. "Is it okay if I smoke *now*?"

The inspector shrugged. "Be my guest."

As Emile strode toward the door, pulling his cigarettes from the pocket of his jeans, a grubby envelope fell to the floor behind him. Andrew stooped and picked it up, but before he could return it, Emile had gone. Andrew stared at the envelope, then showed it to us. On the front it was addressed to Emile Michel Arnaud in care of Euro-Cruises Company, with an address in Paris, but it was the back of the envelope that engaged our attention. In a feminine handwriting was a name, a Paris address, and the dates "June 10 to 24."

Now I remembered where I had seen this envelope before. It was the past Sunday evening, the first night of the cruise. We were in the café on the bank above the spot where the boat was moored. Emile and Marie sat at a nearby table, and Emile brought out a grubby envelope for Marie to write her name and address.

The next two hours were a busy time at the police station in Tournus. Inspector Moreau made a series of phone calls, some to Paris and to other parts of France, some abroad. When all the information was assembled, he sat back and shook his head. "It is possible that we have the answer," he said with some irritation, "but we have no proof."

In the silence that followed, Andrew began to whistle softly and a fragment of Mozart floated in the air. I could see that Andrew was so absorbed in thought that he was quite unaware of the sound he produced.

The inspector and I exchanged a smile and waited.

Then Andrew emerged from his trance to say, "I have an idea. There is no guarantee that it will help, but I think it can do no harm."

When he had explained his plan, the inspector pondered. At last he said, "We may as well give it a try. As you say, if it produces no results, at least nothing is lost. About half past nine, then? It will be getting dark soon after that."

When they had settled the final details, Andrew and I set off for the boat with time to spare before dinner.

Back on the *Jacqueline*, I stepped gratefully into the tiny shower. Ellen and I agreed that decent pants and sweaters were sufficient dress for dinner—it was hardly a festive occasion.

While my friend tactfully refrained from asking me what had transpired at the police station that day, I told her a good deal of what had taken place. "We're all to assemble at nine-thirty tonight and you'll hear most of it from Andrew anyway. He's going to be the formal speaker!"

Ellen gave me a direct look from her green eyes, her expression thoughtful. "Andrew is an exceptional person, isn't he, Jane?"

My heart gave a little leap, but I repressed any impulse toward girlish enthusiasm and answered quietly. "He's a very dear man, yes."

Ellen said no more, but when we went above and were standing in the salon with our drinks, I saw Andrew move to Ellen's side as if he belonged there, and their talk was as comfortable as that of two very old friends.

I glided away and found myself beside Stephen, who muttered, "Oh, hello, darling." I had moved up another notch in his esteem, I noticed. "How dreadful," he went on, "being questioned by the police as if one were a criminal, or at least a suspect. Quite gruesome. Did I do well, dear?"

He sounded so much like an actor who wants an opinion on his performance that I smiled. "Have you ever done any acting, Stephen?"

"Oh, only in a small way, but I'm saving my money and I intend to have another go at the theater."

"I thought you did very well," I said, an answer which I thought covered all contingencies.

At a quarter to seven Philippe was tasting the soup for his first course, and Stephen was drawing the corks from bottles of wine, when suddenly we heard the sound of voices shouting in anger.

It was Marie and Emile, on the crew's deck beyond the galley.

"You *what?*" Marie shouted.

"I said, I told them to look up your goddamn boyfriend on the motorcycle and leave me alone!"

"You beast! You rotten beast!" From the salon we could hear the clear sound of a slap.

Then Emile's voice snarled, "Don't you hit me, you bitch!" There was a blow and a scream, and a thud as Marie evidently fell to the deck.

Andrew and Don dashed through the galley, Ellen and I behind them. I could see Marie lying against the bulkhead, blood streaming from the side of her head, while Stephen and Philippe held a struggling Emile by the arms.

"I'll kill her, the little bitch," Emile was shouting.

The policeman who had been stationed at the foot of the gangplank now leapt aboard and traversed the outside walkway in a few strides, Emile subsiding into a chair at sight of the officer.

Philippe produced a damp cloth and pressed it against the cut on Marie's head, but it was quickly apparent that Marie was bleeding profusely.

"Look," said Andrew to Don, "there's a police car by the bridge. I think she may need some stitches. Go ahead with dinner and I'll take her up. Just keep a plate for me, okay?" Don agreed.

The policeman looked at Andrew, whom he had seen at the station and assumed to be in authority. "Shall I take him in, sir?" he asked, indicating Emile.

"No, he's all right here for now. We can ask the inspector later on. While you are on the quay no one can leave the boat."

The policeman went back to his post at the foot of

the gangplank and Andrew took Marie to the waiting police car. Having obtained permission from the station, the driver took them up the hill to the hospital, where Andrew, describing the event afterward, said he felt he was becoming an habitué.

While the doctor on duty was treating Marie, Andrew stood thinking for a few moments, then went down the hall and spoke with the laboratory technician. Next, he placed a call to the police station, catching Moreau as he prepared to leave for dinner.

After telling the inspector about the injury to Marie, Andrew added, "This is a question that didn't arise at the time Poppa was here in the hospital. Since I happen to be here, there's something I should like to check out." He asked if the inspector would telephone the lab technician and make a certain request.

"Yes, by all means," replied the inspector. "I'll see you at nine-thirty on the *Jacqueline*."

22

The warm sunshine of the afternoon had disappeared under a layer of cloud by the time Andrew brought Marie back to the *Jacqueline*. We had finished our dinner and Ellen and I were out on the deck when they arrived. I saw Marie shiver as she stepped onto the deck, and Andrew put his coat around her shoulders.

Marie looked at him gratefully. "I don't usually feel the cold."

Ellen said, "You probably have a bit of shock. Are you sure you're all right?"

"Oh, yes, I'm fine."

But we noticed that the usually spirited Marie was subdued and brooding, holding her bandaged head and walking unsteadily through the salon toward the crew's quarters. Then Philippe appeared with Andrew's dinner, and we left him to eat in peace.

Everyone on board had been asked to be present in the salon at nine-thirty. At quarter after nine I glanced out and saw that things were going according to plan.

The police car that had been stationed near the bridge on the road above the *Jacqueline* drove off into the town. A few moments later a small, nondescript automobile pulled into the same spot and a man in working clothes got out and stood looking out over the river, smoking a cigarette and glancing at his watch from time to time as if he were waiting for someone.

Then Inspector Moreau appeared and walked down to the quay, speaking to the policeman on duty at the foot of the gangplank. When the inspector had gone aboard, the policeman went quietly up the gangplank, crossed the deck, and stepped along the walkway on the far side of the boat, standing against a bulkhead, where he could not be seen by anyone on the boat or on the quay.

As the guests and crew members came into the salon, they were placed in a sort of rough semicircle, facing the dining area. The guests occupied the two plush-covered seating areas on either side of the cabin—Molly, Ellen, Don, and Julie on one side, with Rosanna, Tonio, Karl, and I on the opposite side.

The crew members sat in chairs that extended the circle. Emile took the chair at Julie's left, while Philippe went to the other side and sat at my right. When Marie came into the salon, Emile gestured to the chair next to his, but she merely gave him a murderous look and walked over to sit beside me. The inspector quietly slipped into the chair next to Emile, while Andrew pulled up a chair in the center and asked everyone for attention.

The only person not seated was Stephen Shaw, who stood leaning against the door that led outside from the salon to the observation deck. Andrew gave him a quick glance but said nothing.

"Messieurs and mesdames," the inspector began, "we have asked you to assemble here to talk with you about the tragic events which have occurred on what was expected to be a cruise of pleasure. My old friend Andrew Quentin has been most helpful to me today and I have asked him to speak to you on my behalf, since my English is not of the best. Please be assured that what he has to say has my full authority and support. Thank you.''

Andrew cleared his throat and looked around at the faces obediently turned to face him. He told me afterward it felt exactly like the first meeting of a class at the university, even to the sheaf of notes in his hand. All he needed was a lectern to feel at home.

''Inspector Moreau would like all of you to know at once that he does not have a final solution to the apparent crimes that have occurred this week. If he did so, the guilty person or persons would by now be under arrest. The purpose of this gathering is to inform you of the present status of the inquiry in the hope that some further information may be forthcoming. One of you might remember something that is pertinent or be willing to give information that was previously withheld. In any case, I shall proceed by taking you step by step through the various theories that have brought us up to the present moment.

''We have the possibility of three crimes. The most recent, the attack on Molly O'Connor which took place last evening in the crypt of the Abbey here in Tournus, was undeniably an assault, and from its severity it appears that the intention was murder. Fortunately, the attacker stopped short, no doubt believing that the deed was accomplished. Second, we have physical evidence that strongly indicates that Poppa O'Connor's death was not the result of an accidental overdose of his medicine but that it was caused by someone intentionally making it likely that he would ingest more than his usual dose and hence would die. Third, in the light of O'Connor's death, it now seems probable that Poppa was pushed into the canal on Monday evening, as he himself insisted, and that whoever pushed him may have intended that he would drown or that the shock would result in a fatal attack to his already damaged heart.

"Now, if all three of these events were intentional crimes, it is possible that they were all committed by the same person or that one or more of the crimes was committed by different persons.

"As Inspector Moreau would be the first to tell you, police work is not a matter of mystique. The police proceed in most cases with the same common sense that laymen would apply to the problems facing them. That is to say, they look for motive and opportunity. Who had any reason to bring harm or death to the victims, and did those persons have the chance to do so?

"In the present case, most of you here tonight had the opportunity to commit some or all of the crimes. You may say that both the attack on Molly and the incident at the canal could have been done by a total stranger, and that is true. Pushing Poppa into the canal might have been a senseless prank. There were people from other barges and from the houses in the area who were milling about at the time the lock was being repaired. Similarly, Molly's attacker could have been a mugger who was frightened away before he could take the considerable sum of money which was still in her purse.

"However, when we come to the most serious of the crimes, the death of Poppa O'Connor, the possibility of an outsider gaining access to his cabin and knowing about his medicine becomes a near impossibility. Therefore, Inspector Moreau began his inquiry with the question of first importance: Who would want Poppa O'Connor dead?

"Assembling the evidence from the interviews that were held with all of you today, it was clear that the most powerful motive for his murder was connected with the matter of who would inherit, or share in the inheritance, of Poppa's considerable fortune.

"However, before addressing the matter of the inheritance, I must point out that at least two persons on board the *Jacqueline* held strong feelings of resentment against Poppa O'Connor for reasons unrelated to the matter of the inheritance.

"Most of the guests are aware of the quarrel between Rosanna Rossi and Poppa over a contract for a role at an opera house in England. Poppa himself almost openly accused Rosanna of pushing him into the canal, and as an old friend of Poppa's from many years ago, Rosanna knew that Poppa had never learned to swim. It is possible that she might have impulsively decided to try another prank, as she might think of it, by adding medicine to Poppa's glass, not realizing the full danger of her action.

"If her intent was more serious and she truly intended for Poppa to die, we must then look again at her motive. If Poppa alive might eventually be persuaded to do what she wanted in relation to Glyndebourne, then she would surely not wish him dead. On the other hand, with Poppa gone, the decision would probably fall to Don Hubbard, and she may have counted on getting his cooperation where she had failed with Poppa.

Tonio sprang to his feet. "How can you think such things about the signora? It is dreadful!"

Rosanna pulled him back to his seat. "Never mind, darling, it's only a theory. There's no proof of anything." And she gave Andrew a mocking smile.

Andrew nodded blandly in return and went on. "The other person with cause for resentment against Poppa O'Connor is Miss Julie Bergstrom, and in her case again there is no connection with the question of the inheritance."

Don stirred in his chair. "Really, Andrew, is this necessary—?" But Julie shook her head. "It's all right," she whispered.

Andrew's tone was gentle. "Julie had not met Poppa O'Connor before coming on the cruise this week, but a personal matter, which I need not describe but which related to a member of her family, caused her to nourish a deep resentment against him. Since she was giving a performance in Lyon at the time of the attack on Molly, she is clear of that charge, but her motive against Poppa was a fact that had to be considered.

"Now we may turn to the rather complicated matter of the disposal of Poppa's money to his heirs. Up until Tuesday evening at bedtime, everyone on board, including the crew, was aware that Poppa had refused to make a will and that his son by his first wife might inherit to the exclusion of Molly's children, Don and Ellen, who had never been adopted by Poppa. Thus, Don and Ellen might be said to have had a motive for killing their stepfather.

"However, by the next day it was known that Poppa had changed his mind and had made a will in which all three offspring shared equally. Thus the motive for Don and Ellen to dispose of their stepfather would seem to be eliminated. However, it could have occurred to one or both of them that Poppa's volatile personality could not be depended upon. Suppose he met his son by his first wife and became entranced with the young man. Might he not secretly write another will, invalidating the present one, and leave the bulk of his estate to his own son and little or

176

nothing to his stepchildren? In that case, was it not safer to secure at least a full share in the inheritance while the current will was in effect?''

Molly looked up at Andrew with the fixed and sorrowful expression that she had worn ever since Poppa's death and the attack on herself. "You surely don't believe that Don or Ellen—?"

"No, Molly, no one is making accusations. I'm sure we all understand that the police must consider all possibilities in a case such as this one."

Molly sank back in her chair, staring blankly ahead, her face ashen.

"Apart from the possible role of the stepchildren, a key question arose for the investigation: Where is the son whom Poppa had never seen? Is it possible that he might have seized the opportunity to dispose of Poppa, feeling sure that the death would be regarded as an accident?

"If so, is he by chance aboard the *Jacqueline?*''

23

There was a stir among the circle of listeners aboard the *Jacqueline* when Andrew suggested that Odette's son might be on board.

Tonio leaned toward Rosanna and murmured in her ear, "That is perhaps why the inspector asked me about my parents?"

Julie and Ellen both looked at Don in surprise, but he shook his head. "It's news to me," he said.

Molly simply stared vacantly at Andrew as if she were in a trance.

Andrew looked briefly at the notes in his hand, then went on. "The only facts known to us about the son of Poppa O'Connor are those told to him on the telephone by his former wife, Odette—that she was pregnant at the time she left Poppa, that she returned to France after the divorce, that she remarried after the child was born, and that she named the boy Michel, presumably after Poppa, whose name was Michael. She stated that her husband had died two years ago and that she was living in Paris but did not give Poppa her surname or her address. Of course, we have no way of knowing whether any of the statements made by Odette are true.

"During one of our interviews with Poppa this week, he mentioned that Odette had left him around Christmastime. This was twenty-six years ago, so that the boy would now be twenty-five years old, or very nearly so. Within a range of several months, depending upon whether the mother was already somewhat advanced in the pregnancy or whether the child was conceived very shortly before her departure, the child, if full term, would have been born between May and September of the following year.

"It happens that a number of young men of this age are aboard the *Jacqueline* this week: Tonio Riccardi and Karl Gebler among the guests, and three crew members, Stephĕn Shaw, Philippe Berger, and Emile Arnaud. During the interviews today, Inspector Moreau asked each of these men about his parents, bearing in mind that the answers he received were not necessarily the truth. After the last of the interviews, the inspector placed a series of phone calls to check up on the information he had received, looking for confirmation on the one hand or for evidence of falsehood on the other.

"In the case of Tonio Riccardi, Inspector Moreau spoke on the telephone with his mother in San Remo and she confirmed all the information that Tonio had given. Even if Tonio were not the missing heir, however, there was another possibility that must be considered. As the devoted friend of Rosanna Rossi, Tonio might well share in her anger and indignation over Poppa's refusal to cooperate in the matter of contracts. It is possible that he might have joined with her in perpetrating what was intended as pranks to annoy Poppa and which inadvertently resulted in his death.

This time Tonio sat quietly and made no objection.

"As for Karl Gebler, the inspector was at last able to reach his mother, who is at present visiting her sister in Paris. Madame Gebler, who is a native of France, confirmed what Karl had reported—that her husband was German, that he had died nearly three years ago, and that he had left her well provided for, having been the owner of a lucrative textile company. She denied ever having been to the United States.

"We must assume, of course, that if either Madame Riccardi or Madame Gebler were indeed the first wife of Poppa O'Connor, she would have been informed by her son of what has taken place this week and would not wish to disclose her identity until the matter of Poppa's death has been cleared up. If necessary, the police will continue their investigation of these facts."

Karl Gebler gave a snort of disgust. "It is ridiculous. There is nothing to find out."

Ignoring this outburst, Andrew went on. "When we come to the members of the crew, the inspector's task was made easier by the fact that the Euro-Cruises company has information on file for its employees. He spoke to the housekeeper at Stephen Shaw's home in London, who confirmed that Stephen's parents are traveling in New Zealand. This information will also be further checked against the possibility that the housekeeper was merely acting under instructions.

"As for our talented chef," Andrew went on, giving a slight nod toward Philippe, "the records confirm that he was already twenty-six in January and thus could not be the son of Odette. However, what he told us at his interview posed some interesting problems. First, he mentioned that after luncheon yesterday he noticed Marie and the captain looking at a large sheet of yellow paper, which Emile quickly folded and put into his shirt pocket when Philippe approached. Jane—Dr.

Winfield—recalled seeing two large tablets—one yellow and the other white—in the O'Connors' cabin when Molly was searching for a magazine for her. When the magazine was found, it was under the two writing tablets.

"When the tablets were brought into the police station as requested, the technician identified portions of what had been written on the preceding page of each by tracing the pressure made by the ball-point pen."

Andrew held up two sheets of paper. "Here are photocopies of the sheets in question. From the fragments of words which appear, it is clear that these are both copies of Poppa O'Connor's will, one in his handwriting and the other in another hand."

Walking across the salon, Andrew gently handed the two sheets to Molly.

"Do you recognize these?"

Molly looked at the sheets and then slowly raised her eyes to Andrew's. "Yes," she said quietly, "I wrote it out and he copied it." Her soft brown eyes filled with tears as she gave the sheets back to Andrew.

"Thank you," he said, returning to his seat. "If the yellow paper seen by Philippe was the original of Molly's copy of the will, then it would be easy enough to conjecture that Marie had found it while doing up the cabins the next morning and had decided to keep it for further study. I have meanwhile asked both Marie and Emile about this and both have denied that the paper Philippe saw had anything to do with the will. We shall return to this question in a moment.

"Meanwhile, Philippe gave us another bit of puzzling information. He reported that at about a quarter of three yesterday afternoon, he heard Rosanna Rossi singing here on the boat, and that the sound seemed to come from below, probably from her cabin.

Rosanna states that she did not return to the boat until half past three, a fact confirmed by Tonio, who was waiting for her. Of course, it was possible for her to return to the boat at a quarter to three, leave, and return again later.

"As you all know, the hours between two and four-thirty yesterday afternoon comprise the time when someone may have entered Poppa's cabin and dropped extra tablets of medicine into his wine, thus causing his death. Each of you has been asked to account for your movements at that time. Therefore, it is important to resolve the conflicting stories of Philippe and Rosanna.

"With that in mind, I am going to try a little experiment to see if we can solve the problem. First of all, Philippe, can you tell us what the music the lady was singing sounded like?"

Philippe looked uncomfortable. "I don't know much about opera and all that."

"That's all right. Did it sound like scales?"

"I don't know."

Andrew looked at Rosanna. "Please, will you do a few scales and runs?"

With a shrug Rosanna rippled a series of practice runs, her voice moving up smoothly from one register to another and back down again.

"Did it sound like that?" Andrew asked.

Philippe shook his head. "No, not at all. I hear Madame singing that way in the morning. This was different."

Andrew walked over to a shelf where he had placed his tape recorder. Taking out a cassette, he checked the label, inserted the cassette, and pressed the button for play. In a moment a soprano voice filled the room with long sustained tones floating over a low orchestral accompaniment.

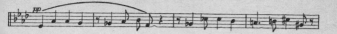

Philippe listened, then nodded vigorously. "Yes, yes! I do not know if it is the same music, but it was just like that—long and slow. Very beautiful!"

Rosanna looked indignant. "But I've never sung that in my life!" she exclaimed.

Andrew smiled at her. "Exactly. I think we have just proved that you were not singing here on the boat at a quarter of three yesterday!"

24

Ignoring the puzzled looks of some of his listeners after his music experiment, Andrew continued his discourse.

"That brings us to the captain, Emile Arnaud. Just moments before Emile came into the police station to be interviewed this afternoon, we saw for the first time the printed list of crew members which Stephen Shaw had handed to Inspector Moreau earlier today. Noting that the captain's full name was Emile Michel Arnaud, we saw the possibility that Odette might have given the child the name Michel as a middle, not a given, name."

Emile leaned back in his chair, stretching his legs full-length before him, and gave Andrew an insolent smile. "You're crazy!"

"Therefore, it was with particular interest that the inspector questioned him. Emile's age—he had turned twenty-five just now, in the month of June—fit the possibility that he was the missing son. He had been near the lock on Monday evening, although he claimed that he was on the opposite side of the canal.

"Yesterday afternoon he had had ample opportunity to enter Poppa's cabin after the guests had gone and before meeting Marie in the town. As for last evening, he was seen in the vicinity of the Abbey at the time of the attack on Molly. We have only his word that he did not go inside.

"There is another significant factor in the case of Emile, and that is his propensity for violence. We have all seen what happened to Marie this evening, and I have reason to believe it's not the first time he has struck her."

"Aw, shit!" Emile snorted. "That's nothing. Women like to be knocked around."

Andrew allowed this statement to hang in frozen silence for a moment, then went calmly on.

"This brings us to the question of the attack on Molly. Physically, anyone might push an old man into a canal or drop some tablets into his wine, but the person who attempted to murder Molly must have had some innate capacity for physical violence. It's true that anyone, under severe pressure of emotion, might be capable of an act of violence that would normally be unthinkable, but we are not dealing here with a heated quarrel or a moment of passion. This is someone who saw Molly go down into the crypt, who quietly followed her, who hid in an aperture of the wall, and who lured her into a position where she could be violently attacked.

"But why? Why Molly? This is the question that no one seemingly could answer. If the attacker was not a stranger, what motive could anyone have for wanting Molly out of the way?

"And now we became aware of a crucial difference in the testimony of the young men who had been questioned. Each one was asked what he believed to be the contents of the will Poppa had made on Tuesday evening. Philippe did not know, but Tonio, Karl, and Stephen all stated their belief that the money was to be shared equally with what we might call Poppa's three children—that is, his own son and his stepchildren, Don Hubbard and Ellen Walker.

"But when Emile was questioned we got a different answer. He said he knew only what everyone was saying—that Poppa's money *'would go first to his wife and then to his three kids.'*

"But this was not in fact what *'everyone was saying.'* No one else had mentioned that Molly would have the entire estate for her lifetime, with the remainder going to the heirs after her death. In fact, Poppa told me himself about his will the next morning, simply saying that he had left equal shares to the three children. Apparently neither he nor Molly regarded her life estate as worth mentioning, since the controversy had involved the question of inheritance for the younger generation.

"But how did Emile know these facts about the will? Obviously, the yellow sheet that Emile and Marie were so interested in reading was in fact Molly's draft of the will, which she had shown to her daughter and her friend Jane that evening and then dropped into their wastebasket, where it was found by Marie the next morning.

"Now it was clear that Odette's son, whoever he might be, had a strong motive for killing Molly. You wouldn't have to be a lawyer to figure out that if Molly was dead, Poppa's entire estate would be divided among the three heirs. There would be no waiting, perhaps for years, for Molly to die. Better to strike now. It was risky, but even if he were suspected, no one could prove anything."

Now Emile roared. "You're not going to pin this fucking murder on me!"

Smoothly, Andrew went on. "When the inspector continued his questioning of Emile, we were further disturbed that Emile refused to divulge his mother's address. Afterward, however, Inspector Moreau reached an uncle of Emile in Marseille, whose address was listed with Euro-Cruises and learned that a—er—personal matter could explain his refusal."

Emile had glared wildly at Andrew's first mention of his mother but subsided at once with his subsequent statement. Andrew saw no reason to disclose what the inspector had in fact learned—that Emile's mother was a prostitute in Montmartre. For all his toughness, it was apparent that Emile wanted desperately to keep the circumstances of his mother's life a secret.

"At the end of the interview with Emile in the police station this afternoon, he rather spitefully suggested that the inspector might find a better suspect in a mysterious man on a motorcycle whom he had seen Marie meeting at various times during the cruise.

"Emile apparently did not know that we had already questioned Marie this morning about this person and that she had described him as a friend from Paris who had once been in trouble with the police and therefore did not want to be identified.

"Marie stated that her friend had returned to Paris, but the inspector dispatched an officer to see if he could locate the man. In a town the size of Tournus it was child's play to learn that he was still here and to find the hotel where he was staying on the outskirts of town. It was equally easy to lift a set of fingerprints from the handle of his motorbike. These were sent to the central clearing office in Paris, but so far no evidence of a prior arrest has been found.

"Our first assumption about this man was that he

might be the son of Poppa and Odette and that he had enlisted Marie to become acquainted with someone on the *Jacqueline* so that he could obtain information about Poppa and his circumstances.

"However, an incident occurred as Emile left the interrogation room which offered a different theory.

"In pulling out his pack of cigarettes, Emile dropped a crumpled envelope on the floor. I picked it up and saw that it was addressed to Emile at the office of Euro-Cruises. On the back I saw something startling. In a feminine handwriting was the name Marie Michèle Dupont. This was followed by the Paris address which Marie had given us that morning and two dates in June. Evidently here was the information given to the captain by Marie last Sunday evening to obtain approval for her to work on the boat.

"Marie Michèle. Was it possible that the child born to Odette was a daughter, not a son? Had she actually told Poppa that the child was a boy or had he merely assumed that it was so because of the name he heard on the telephone as 'Michel'?"

I looked at Marie and saw her staring at Andrew with terror in her eyes.

"Now," he went on, "the role of the mystery man on the motorcycle might be reversed. He might be Marie's accomplice. All of the motives for disposing of Poppa and Molly were the same for a daughter of Poppa as for a son, and if the dangerous tasks were performed by someone who was never identified, then Marie herself was in no danger.

"It could have been this young man who pushed Poppa into the canal and who made the attack on Molly. And, following Marie's directions, he could have entered the boat, found Poppa's cabin, and dropped the medicine into his wineglass while Poppa slept."

Suddenly Andrew raised his voice and proclaimed dramatically, "Now, however, the police have the fingerprints of this man and he can be picked up at any time!"

Andrew looked at Stephen Shaw, where he stood in the doorway to the deck. Suddenly Stephen darted out of the door and the sounds of a scuffle were heard. The inspector leapt to his feet and made for the door, while the rest of the group sat in stunned silence staring at the doorway.

Then the inspector came back into the salon and behind him came the figures of Stephen Shaw and a uniformed policeman. Struggling between them was a slender man in a black turtleneck sweater with a stocking cap pulled well down over his ears, and a little dark mustache on his upper lip.

"Over here," said the inspector, indicating the chair he had just vacated.

The man finally ceased to struggle and sat down sullenly.

With an enigmatic smile the inspector said, "Here is our mystery man on the motorcycle." Then he turned to Andrew with a gesture that said, Your turn.

Andrew bent over the man in the chair, staring at him intently. Then, with a quick movement, he pulled the mustache with one hand and the stocking cap with the other.

Marie gasped and cried out, "No! No!"

Andrew stepped back to reveal a woman with short brown hair who glared at him venomously.

To the circle of astonished faces, Andrew said, "May I present Madame Odette Dupont, the former wife of Poppa O'Connor!"

25

The next day, Friday, which should have been a day of triumph for Inspector Moreau, became, instead, one of maddening frustration. Odette and Marie had both been held overnight for questioning, but neither had spoken a word, except to deny everything, Marie following her mother's instructions not to open her mouth until their lawyer arrived from Paris the following morning. Since the police had no hard evidence against them, the lawyer secured their release and whisked them back to Paris, where they were warned to remain available.

Andrew and I spent another day at the police station, while each of the guests and crew were interviewed again in the hope that new information would turn up relating to Odette and her activities. Signed statements were taken from each one, but after hours of painstaking work, nothing new emerged.

By late afternoon all of us who were guests on the *Jacqueline* agreed that we may as well spend the last night on the boat and return to Paris the next day, as originally scheduled.

"No use missing another of Philippe's dinners," as Rosanna put it flippantly.

When the others had returned to the boat, Andrew and I sat with the inspector over a pitcher of wine at a café near the police station.

Moreau pulled at his mustache. "I am as certain as one can be that Madame Odette is guilty of these crimes, but what can one do? We have absolutely no concrete evidence against her."

"Yes," Andrew said. "She has all the motive in the world, and we can place her at the scene in all three incidents."

Moreau nodded. "Exactly. You remember that the violinist fellow said he was nearly knocked down by a rider on a motorcycle along the towpath of the canal before the old man went into the water? The Poppa told his wife he heard the sound of a motorcycle, and others think they heard it as well. So what does that prove? Absolutely nothing. A dozen riders might be cluttering up the towpath at the same time, but no one sees our lady in disguise!"

"The motive was there," I added. "At that time Marie would have reported to her mother that Poppa had not made a will, and Odette would have liked to dispose of him before he could make one and perhaps leave only a token to his child by her. Then, when they learn that the will is made, it becomes desirable to get rid of Molly."

"Yes." Andrew moved restlessly. "It's so irritating that after the attack on Molly, I saw Odette myself outside the Abbey minutes later. Emile was shouting at 'the man' to stop, and she tore off on the motorbike. But again, it proves nothing."

The inspector sighed. "As for giving the medicine

to the Poppa, she could have entered the boat at any time that afternoon. However, people were coming and going until after three o'clock. Then Tonio was standing on the deck until three-thirty. Her best chance would have been after that, except that the two singers were playing cards in the salon and would have seen her going down the stairs.''

''But there is a way,'' Andrew said. ''She need not go down the stairs. Remember the ladder from the deck that comes out near Poppa's cabin? Marie has told her everything about the boat. She sees that no one is visible. She steps onto the deck and hears the voices of Rosanna and Tonio as they play cards. But they cannot see the cube on the deck which gives entrance to the ladder. She slips down the ladder, finds Poppa asleep, quickly drops some tablets into his glass and fills it from the decanter, using a tissue to avoid leaving fingerprints. Back up the ladder and no one the wiser.''

''But, alas! How to prove it?''

Andrew laughed ruefully. ''That was what my great experiment was intended for. On a television show the culprit always breaks down and confesses, and that was exactly what I hoped Odette would do. From everything we had heard about her, it seemed possible. Poppa called her 'wild and crazy,' and certainly her attempt to strangle Molly indicates a violent and probably unstable personality. I thought my dramatic scene might work, but it didn't. I'm surprised that she hasn't broken down.''

The inspector grumbled, ''She is a smart cookie, that one. Hard as nails. Unfortunately, so long as she refuses to speak, we can do nothing. Yes, she was at the scene of each crime, but so were half a dozen others. I shall leave the case open, of course, but it is of no use to bring her to trial if we have nothing concrete against her."

We sipped our wine in depressed silence for a while. Then Andrew said, "We may as well be off."

The inspector thanked me warmly for my help in translation, then said to Andrew, "I'll call for you in half an hour."

They had arranged that Andrew would go back to Lyon with his friend, spending the night with Moreau and his family and boarding the same train in Lyon the next morning that our group would later join in Dijon.

Our last evening on the *Jacqueline,* while tinged with melancholy over Poppa's death, was an occasion of greater cheer than the evening before, as everyone rejoiced at being freed from suspicion. Molly, of course, could not be expected to share in the general high spirits. Back in the cabin she had shared with Poppa she had her dinner on a tray and asked not to be disturbed.

"I've given her a sleeping pill," Ellen told me. "She desperately needs her rest."

In the salon Karl Gebler almost managed a smile as he proclaimed his relief. "Of course, it was absurd to suspect me of these crimes. I admired Mr. O'Connor and his wife and had no wish to harm them. Besides, even if I had been the missing son, I would never risk my career by committing a murder merely for an inheritance!"

Don smiled. "Poor Momma—she looked so terrified when she thought Ellen and I might be suspects."

Rosanna's rich voice surged up. "I'm glad it was Odette that pushed poor old Poppa into the canal. I was sorely tempted to do it myself, I can tell you. But I did begin to wonder about you, Tonio darling. I've never met your parents. Your mother might have had a lurid past you knew nothing about!"

Tonio merely looked at her with sorrowful eyes. "Ah, Signora, you must not joke about such things."

Apart from the others, I heard Don say to Julie, "I didn't like it when Andrew suggested you might be a suspect."

Her beautiful face lighted in a rare smile. "Oh, Don, thank you. At least, he didn't have to explain about what happened to my brother."

At the end of the evening, Stephen Shaw asked me to join him in a nightcap.

"You've been such a brick, Jane." I couldn't see that I had done anything but listen, but maybe that's what he needed.

Fingering his gold chain, he went on. "I was so pleased when the inspector asked me to play my little part in the charade last night. I had no idea what it was all about, except that I was to watch for a person who might come aboard and appear to be listening outside the salon. But how on earth did he know that the mystery person on the motorcycle would turn up on the boat?"

"Well, Stephen, I don't think anyone knew for sure, but once we had worked out that Marie was Odette's daughter, it seemed likely that the stranger she was meeting must have some connection with what was going on. Andrew suggested that the police car on the quay be replaced by a plainclothes officer in an unmarked car and that the policeman at the foot of the gangplank be instructed to remain out of sight on the other side of the boat. Since Odette—as we now know it was—had been lurking around constantly, the assumption was that she would see the gathering in the salon, would believe that the police guard had been removed, and would come down to listen. If she didn't come down to the boat, the officer on the quay was to follow her.''

"I see. My signal was simply to watch for a fleeing figure when Andrew raised his voice and said something about fingerprints. She must have sneaked aboard while I wasn't looking, because I was totally startled when, right on cue, I saw what I took to be a young man making a leap for the gangplank. We had no trouble cutting her off, but she did rather put up a struggle!''

"You were splendid, Stephen,'' I said, and we bid each other a cordial good night.

On the journey back to Paris on the train the next day, Andrew joined up with us, reporting a pleasant visit with his friends at Lyon the evening before.

As we neared Paris, Ellen and I shared our sense of relief that the worst of the ordeal of the past week was over, when an incident occurred which further lightened our mood. Andrew returned from a visit to the buffet car and invited us to stand with him at the back of the car, where the sound of the train muffled our voices.

Smiling broadly, he proceeded to tell us about his recent encounters in the buffet.

"I saw Tonio sitting alone at a little table at the far end of the car and I thought, he must be trying to escape the clutches of the Iron Lady for a little while, but I soon learned how wrong I was. When I remarked that Rosanna was still a most attractive woman, Tonio responded with that wonderful assumption of the Italian that one's love life is a topic of absorbing interest.

" 'Ah, the signora!' he said to me with a sigh. 'She is marvelous! She has had so many husbands—so many lovers—yet she makes me feel that I am the best. I know she has probably said the same to all of them but yet she makes me feel—how do you say it?—glorious! With the young girls it is so tiresome. It is, "Hurry up, Toni," or "Don't muss my hair." But the signora—how I adore her. I know she is growing bored with me. She never says so but I feel it. Yet I worship her!'

"I smiled and said, 'Then you will give up Glyndebourne if she doesn't get the role of Mimi?'

"And he looked at me with astonishment and said, 'Give up Glyndebourne? But that is business. What has that to do with love?'

"No sooner had he gone than Rosanna came into the buffet and, seeing me alone, took a seat at my table, saying 'Hello, darling,' in that wonderfully throaty voice.

"I asked if I could get her something from the buffet, and she asked for a glass of wine. When I returned with two glasses, she raised hers and said, 'To Wagner!'

"I laughed and said, 'I must say, Philippe had me worried for a while. He was so obviously incapable of inventing the story of hearing you singing. It seemed to me he must really have heard *something.*' Then I remembered that bit of the 'Liebestod' from *Tristan und Isolde* was on my tape. I had taped it one day to use in a class at the university, and I had decided not to erase it.

"She reminded me that it had floated out one day when we were interviewing poor Poppa and she had asked if it was Flagstad singing.

"I said, 'Exactly. So on the day Poppa died, someone was in my cabin listening to my tapes.'

"We agreed that we had no idea who it could have been. Then I asked, 'So, Rosanna, what will you do about Glyndebourne? Will Don put up a fight for you?'

"She just smiled and said, 'To tell you the truth,

I've been thinking and I've decided it isn't worth
bothering about. I was furious with Poppa because I
felt he had betrayed me. We had had our tiffs about
this and that, but he had never refused me anything I
really wanted. I think now that he was much sicker
than any of us realized. He had always loved a fight,
and for him to avoid one should have told me that he
was weakening fast.'

"So Tonio can have the role of Rodolfo?"

" 'Of course. I would never have held out to the
point where he lost the part. I just wanted Poppa to
try some leverage.'

"You are really fond of Tonio?"

" 'Yes, he is a dear boy.'

"I noticed that you were angry the other day when
he was flirting with Julie.

" 'Oh, darling, he was just being Italian. No Italian
can resist flirting with a pretty girl. It didn't mean a
thing. But if I didn't make a show of jealousy, the poor
angel would be crushed.'

"Then she bent forward and put her hand over my
arm in a confidential gesture. 'You see, dear, the
problem with Tonio is that he is so serious. If he had
even a glimmer of a sense of humor I'd adore him
forever, but those dark eyes are so solemn. I know it's
dreadful, but sometimes I have to refrain from breaking into giggles at the most inappropriate moments!' "

Ellen and I joined in Andrew's merriment, and I
said, "So much for our theories about other people's
love lives!"

26

An hour later I had just settled into my room at the Meurice when the phone rang. To my surprise, it was Marie, asking if she might talk to me, as there was something worrying her. I agreed to take a taxi to her place, and she gave me an address in Montparnasse.

Before leaving, I called Andrew. "If she asks certain questions, how shall I answer?"

"Use your judgment, Jane. Whatever you decide is fine with me."

When Marie opened the door of her tiny apartment, she offered me some coffee, poured a mug for each of us, and sat down on a daybed opposite my chair. Speaking with her in French to make her feel more at ease, I looked at her bandaged head and asked how she was feeling.

"Oh, I'm all right."

"Will you see Emile again?"

"That creep? No way. A little slap may be okay

between friends, but I don't go in for getting really hurt.''

"Are you worried about your mother?"

An odd expression crossed Marie's face. "No, not really. They can't prove anything against her, can they?"

"We don't know that yet. At any time some new evidence may come in that will prove her connection with the crimes. You are very fond of your mother?"

Marie shrugged. "We get along all right.''

"And your father?"

"He died two years ago. I still miss him." No tears, but a slight quiver of the lower lip, which she tried to conceal. "I don't know how he put up with her. She's not easy to live with, you know.''

I decided to take the plunge. "Marie, it does look as if your mother may have committed these crimes. She's the only one who had a reason—except you yourself.''

Marie gave no sign of indignation. She looked back at me and frowned slightly. "You are very kind and I like you," she said to my surprise. "I'll tell you the truth. I really don't know what Maman did or didn't do.''

"She did ask you to try to find out about Poppa O'Connor, didn't she?"

"Yes, I don't mind telling you that, although I would not say it in court. She wanted me to meet someone on the boat and learn anything I could about him.''

"Then the story of your girlfriend in Dijon who sprained her ankle and could not go bicycling with you was invented?"

Marie's mouth turned up in a half smile. "But yes! I knew the inspector didn't believe that one. Anyhow, it was a coincidence that I had the chance to work on the boat, but I was glad because I was curious about

Monsieur O'Connor. I had been really upset when Maman first told me that Papa was not my real father, but then I thought—I loved him just the same, so did it really matter?''

"Your mother told you that Mr. O'Connor might leave you some money in his will?"

"No, she just said that he was very wealthy and we should find out about his family and what he was like.''

"Didn't you wonder why your mother disguised herself as a man when she met you in the vicinity of the cruise?''

"She said she was afraid Michael—that was Monsieur O'Connor—might recognize her. Besides, she liked to do things like that—you know, sort of mysterious or tricky.''

"Marie, there is something I would like to know, off the record of course. On the afternoon of Poppa O'Connor's overdose of medicine, did you go into Andrew's—that is, Dr. Quentin's—cabin about a quarter to three, looking for something?''

Marie looked embarrassed but answered me frankly. "Yes, I did.''

"And you turned on his tape recorder?''

"Yes. Maman had told me to try to listen to what Monsieur O'Connor had said to you on the tape, because it might tell things she wanted to know about his life, and so on. When all the guests went off into the town of Tournus, Emile wanted me to go with him. I told him to go ahead and I would join him in a few minutes. That was my best chance to listen to the tapes.''

"Yes, I understand. So the music that Emile heard was on the tape?''

"Yes, that's right. I found the tape machine. Then I opened the window of the cabin so that if Dr. Quentin should come back I could say that I was checking all the cabins to see that the windows were closed. Then I turned on the tape and the volume was way up on high. The singing came out very loud, and I was so scared I dropped the recorder onto the bed. Then it took me a minute to find the right button to turn it down.

"By that time I was so nervous that I gave up trying to listen to anything else on the tape, so I just put it back on the shelf, closed the window, and left."

I smiled. "We thought it must be something like that."

"I am sorry for going into the cabin. But how did you know it wasn't Madame Rossi when Philippe heard the singing?"

"Because the music he heard was the 'Liebestod'— the 'Love Death'—from *Tristan und Isolde,* and Madame Rossi told us herself one day that she never sings Wagner. Of course, she might have sung a snatch of the music without ever having sung the role, but it was unlikely that she would do that. One day when Andrew was setting the tape for our interview with Poppa, he accidentally played it, just as you did. So then we worked out from the time when Philippe heard the music that it could have been you in the cabin. Thank you for telling me about it."

"But of course." Marie looked at me with a puzzled frown. "Now may I ask you something? How did you and the police know that the person on the motorcycle was my mother?"

"We didn't know positively until she came onto the boat and Andrew saw her at close range. But I had wondered about you, Marie. If the man on the motorcycle was really a lover who meant so much to you, I thought you might have flirted with Emile to gain access to the boat, but it wouldn't have been necessary to—er—"

Marie's little half smile appeared. "Sleep with him? Yes, you're right. I wouldn't have done that!"

"It was then that I wondered if the rider could be your mother. Last evening, when everyone was gathered together on the boat and Andrew was describing the steps in the investigation, the police had learned that the person on the motorcycle had checked out of "his" hotel, but we felt that the man or woman—whichever it was—would not leave Tournus without finding out what was happening. Inspector Moreau arranged for the police to be out of sight, hoping that the person on the motorbike would believe the police had been withdrawn and might venture near, and that is what happened.

"When your mother was brought in and placed in the chair in the lighted salon, Andrew bent over her and saw that his guess was correct. I must confess that our hope had been that she would break down and tell us at least something of what had really happened."

Marie shuddered slightly. "Maman is so—so strange, so hard to understand—"

I bent forward toward the girl. "Now, Marie, I want to ask you something else. When did you first wonder if your mother might be trying to—er—dispose of Poppa and his wife?"

"I didn't! It never occurred to me until the inspector said that the 'man' on the motorcycle might be doing those things!"

"And now?" I looked at her with compassion. "What do you believe now?"

Marie's eyes fell. "I don't know."

Then she raised her eyes and looked directly at me. "Madame Jane, I wanted to see you because I need to ask you a question. Now that Monsieur O'Connor is dead, the will says that his money will be divided among his three children. If Maman really did—I mean, if she is guilty of—you know what I mean. Well, I wouldn't want to take any money. But if I say that I do not want the money, then it would look as if I believe she did it. You see? So, what should I do?''

I looked at her in admiration. ''You are a good girl, Marie. There are not many people in this world who turn down money under any circumstances! Besides, remember that the children do not inherit until after the death of Mrs. O'Connor. However, I have something to tell you which will solve your problem, although not perhaps in the happiest fashion.''

''What is that?''

''I happen to know that you are not in fact the daughter of Michael O'Connor!''

Marie looked at me in astonishment. ''But how could you know that?''

''Do you remember when Andrew took you up to the hospital in Tournus for the stitches on your scalp?''

''Of course.''

''He had seen the envelope from Emile's pocket with your full name—Marie Michèle Dupont—written on it.''

''Yes. I wrote it for him the night the other stewardess was taken ill.''

''Exactly. That was when the inspector and Andrew and I began to wonder if Poppa's heir might be a daughter instead of a son. When you arrived at the hospital, Andrew went into the laboratory and asked the technician if they had a record of Poppa's blood type. It was only the night before that Poppa had died in that very hospital, and the technician said that he had done the typing himself, along with other blood work ordered by the doctor. Then Andrew called Inspector Moreau and asked his permission to request the lab to take a sample of your blood from the wound on your head and check its type also.''

Marie caught her breath. "They did not match?"

"They did not match. Poppa O'Connor could not have been your father."

Marie sighed. "I think I am glad. Poor Maman! Then it was all—" She stopped abruptly.

"All for nothing?" I prompted her gently.

"No, no! I don't know. I don't want to believe it!"

"Is your mother in great need of money?"

"Maman? No, not really. Papa left her some insurance, and she has a good job. But Maman has always been greedy for money. Whatever we had was never enough. And Mr. O'Connor was truly wealthy, wasn't he?"

"Yes, it's a very large estate, I believe. Enough to be a temptation for almost anyone. But not for you, Marie."

When it was time to take my leave, I put my arms around her. "Good luck, my dear!"

27

On the way back to the hotel I thought about my conversation with Marie. When we were on the *Jacqueline* I had thought of her as a sexy little minx, the possible accomplice of a Paris boyfriend who would do anything to further their mutual interests. Now I saw that she was a young woman with her own code of honor, a being far superior to her mendacious and scheming mother. Where did her principles come from? Perhaps from the man who had married Odette when she returned to France as a "widow" and who had loved little Marie, never telling her that she was not his own child.

It was nearly six o'clock when I returned to the Meurice. As I walked through the lobby I saw Julie and Don in evening dress, standing together. Then Don seemed to be saying to her, "Wait here a moment," and Julie sat down on a nearby sofa while Don walked toward the porter's desk. As I approached I saw Julie's eyes follow Don with a look of shy wonder. Then she saw me and broke into a radiant smile.

"Come and sit down, Jane. Don will be right back."

I decided to take advantage of my opportunity, saying, "Julie, there's something I want to ask you about. Remember the night of your recital here in Paris last week? When we were leaving the concert hall Karl said he wanted to walk but then I saw him get into a taxi and drive off. When he was being questioned by the inspector he became furious when asked about this and flatly refused to answer. We thought then he might be concealing his status as the missing son of Poppa and Odette, but now we know that's not the problem. I have a theory about it, but I don't know whether I'm right and I wonder if you know what it was all about?"

"Oh, I can guess. You see, Karl is gay and he's absolutely terrified that if it becomes known, it will affect his career. He was no doubt going to meet a boyfriend here in Paris. I've told him no one cares, but he doesn't believe me. Is that what you suspected?"

"Yes, but I wasn't sure."

We both looked up to see Don standing there with a small floral box tied with a dazzling ribbon bow.

I'd always been fond of Ellen's brother, and now I beamed at them as they went off to their dinner date.

Before going back to my own room, I knocked on Andrew's door, a few steps along the passage. I found him sunk into a chair, looking depressed. I told him about my talk with Marie and her expression of relief on learning that she could not be Poppa's daughter.

"At first," I went on, "I thought she might be simply covering up for her mother, but I honestly believe she has no idea to what extent Odette may be guilty of any of these crimes."

Still, Andrew's doleful look persisted. "While you were gone, Jane, I asked Molly and Ellen if they wanted to go to dinner with me—and you, too, if you like.''

He stopped, staring silently at the carpet. ''Molly's looking dreadful. Have you noticed?''

''Yes, but with Poppa's death and her own injury, I suppose it's not surprising.''

Andrew looked at me, then down again. ''Yes, you're probably right.''

''So,'' I asked, ''are they coming to dinner?''

''No. Molly said she wanted something sent up to her room, but she urged Ellen to go. What about you?''

Without a moment's hesitation I said, ''Oh, thanks, Andrew, but Molly's plan sounds good to me. I'll have a snack in my room and a cozy chat on the phone with James. You and Ellen go along.'' I thought to myself, I may refrain from overt matchmaking, but I'm certainly not going to put up roadblocks in the path of what I hoped was true love.

Andrew was still frowning. ''You know, Jane, Ellen's been worried about her mother's illness of last year.''

''But Dr. McLaren said she was fine, no return of the cancer.''

''I wonder,'' he said.

He looked at his watch. ''It's morning in California.'' As I left the room, I saw him reach for the phone on the table beside him.

A few hours later a scene was taking place on the embankment of the Seine, not far from the Hotel Meurice. I was not there to hear the conversation in person, but with a bit of poetic license tossed in, I can give a pretty close approximation of it from what Don told Ellen afterward.

It seems that after their dinner, Don and Julie were

strolling slowly along by the river, admiring the sprinkle of stars and the half moon which sent its light down through the balmy air.

Don was saying, "When I walked along here last week with my sister and Jane, I hadn't even met you yet, Julie. It's hard to believe I've known you only a week. I actually let Andrew and Jane go to your recital for me last Saturday night, or I would have met you one day sooner!"

"That's right," Julie said softly. "We met the next morning in the lobby of the hotel."

Presently they stopped to lean against the wall and looked down at the river.

"It was a wonderful dinner, Don," Julie said.

Don looked at the lovely face turned up to his and simply gathered her into his arms and kissed her.

"Oh, God, Julie, I love you."

Julie kissed him back but said nothing at all, so Don plodded on. "I know it's too soon to say anything, but I just couldn't help it. I don't expect you to answer, but maybe if we see a lot of each other you might— well, you never can tell—"

Julie still said nothing, but she must have been smiling, only Don didn't look.

Intent on his argument, he went on. "I know I'm so much older than you—eight years is a lot. And of course I've had a lot of girlfriends. In fact, I lived with a girl for four years until she left me."

"She left you?" breathed Julie.

"Yes, I guess she thought I wasn't exciting enough. I'm sort of a homebody."

Don was still looking out at the river. Absorbed in his own reflections, he said, "It's funny, I've always thought that someday I'd like to settle down and have a family and all that, but if you should ever care about me, of course your career would always come first."

Now he heard Julie laughing and turned in surprise to look at her.

"Career?" Julie cried. "Oh, Don, you are too much! I don't want a career! Of course I love music, but I hate all the fighting and scratching and cutthroat competition in that world. Look at what happened to Eric. And look at Karl—so upset because he got only the *silver* medal instead of the gold! No, music will always be a big part of my life, but I'd take home and family any day over a career as a performer."

Then she stopped, frowning mischievously. "Of course, I'd have to find the right person!" And with a delighted giggle she put her arms out to Don.

It was after her own dinner with Andrew that Ellen told me about her brother and Julie. "Don is absolutely walking on air," she reported. "He floated into my room just now, while Julie is changing so they can go for another moonlight stroll. I do think she's right for him, don't you, Jane?"

"Oh, yes! She's a darling."

Ellen smiled. "I knew he adored her at first sight, but Don's always so modest. He can't believe his luck!"

Casually, I said, "So, how was your dinner with Andrew?"

Ellen's green eyes looked directly into mine. "It's odd, Jane. I feel so comfortable with Andrew, as if we've known each other for ages. We can talk about anything that comes into our heads and we seem to understand. He told me he feels the same, that he can talk to me as spontaneously as he did with his wife—which I take to be an enormous compliment."

I nodded. "That's a rare tribute, I think."

A slight flush tinged her fair skin. "He told me that a week ago he had wanted to go to the restaurant where we dined tonight but he couldn't face it because he had been there with Norma when they were in Paris. Then he discovered that he wanted to take me there—and it had been a wonderful evening for him."

"I think that's rather special, Ellen. I know Andrew has dated women from time to time since his wife died, but there's never been a serious relationship."

"I understand that, because it describes about where I am now. I'm not at all ready for a serious thing with anyone—it's too soon. You know, Jane, sometimes I think marriage is a kind of lottery. Two people fall in love and the lucky ones, like you and James, or Andrew and his wife, grow together, while Joe and I simply grew away from each other. It was never a case of who was right or wrong, yet it was painful for both of us."

I nodded, remembering a wretched love affair I had suffered through in pre-Jamesian days.

Ellen sighed. "That's what Poppa couldn't understand. You remember what a fuss he made when Joe and I first separated. He insisted that it was my duty as a wife to make the best of everything, and of course what made it so hard for me was that I felt with a part of me that he was right. What surprised me was that Momma supported me completely. Since she was so exactly the kind of wife Poppa described, I had thought she would agree with him. But she said to me, 'Why does everyone always assume it's the wife who must put up with everything? We never hear about the husband's duty to put up with anything!'

"Of course, when Joe found someone else, Poppa was furious. He thought I should fight to get him back and could never understand that I think it's better this way for both of us."

I held my breath. "So, will you be seeing Andrew again at home?"

Ellen's face glowed. "Oh, yes, lots of Thursdays!"

"Really?"

"Yes, we both have season tickets to the Los Angeles Philharmonic that night."

"But, Ellen, isn't the season over for the summer?"

She laughed. "Don't worry. There's always the Hollywood Bowl!"

28

When Ellen had gone back to her room, I was surprised to hear my phone ring at that late hour, and more surprised when I heard Molly's voice. "Jane, dear, I've just said good night to Ellen, so I know she's no longer with you."

"Yes, she left a few minutes ago."

Molly sounded troubled. "I wonder if you would mind coming to my room? I've asked Andrew too. And please say nothing to Ellen."

"Of course, Molly."

When I arrived, Andrew was already there. Molly indicated that I should sit beside him on a small sofa, while she sat in a low chair facing us, her soft brown eyes solemn.

"I'm so sorry to burden you with this, but someone must know, and I feel I can rely on you both."

I felt a flash of alarm, and suddenly all sorts of things began to take shape in my mind. Molly looking for a magazine for me in their cabin on the boat. Molly's odd behavior since Poppa's death. Her terrible fear, that evening on the boat when Andrew was reviewing the events of the case, when she thought Don or Ellen might be suspected of the crime. Andrew's phone call before dinner this evening.

Now Molly looked at Andrew. "How much do you know?"

"I don't really *know* anything, Molly," he said gently, "but I may have guessed."

"That I killed Poppa?"

"Yes."

"Oh, Molly!" I breathed.

"Yes, dear, it's true. I thought Andrew suspected this evening."

Andrew looked surprised. "How did you—?"

"It was the way you looked at me before you and Ellen went out—sort of puzzled but compassionate."

"I see. But *why,* Molly? That's what baffles me. Why Poppa? You were so devoted to him."

"Devoted? Yes, it looked that way to the world, I know. But does anyone really stay 'devoted' to such a monster of egotism as Poppa?"

Andrew said, "I don't know. You had me fooled."

"Remember that I was an actress before I married Poppa. I could have had a pleasant little career and I would have enjoyed that. With his contacts he could easily have helped me along to get small parts, but no—Poppa O'Connor's wife must have no separate existence. Either I became his handmaiden and slave or I would end as Odette did, by leaving him. And I had two small children to protect."

I said, "Did you marry him, then, for his money?"

"No, Jane, that would have made it easy. As it was, I fell for his charm. It had been a terrible shock when my husband died. He was only thirty-two and just getting started in his law practice. I thought I would never marry again, and then Poppa came along and I was totally captivated. When we were married I was really in love with him.

"Then, little by little, it all began to crumble. In the early years he was unfaithful in irritating ways. He always insisted that he never went to bed with other women but he would have obvious 'crushes' on women who chased after him, and that hurt me more than if he had had an occasional fling that I knew nothing about. More than that, in every aspect of his life I learned that he was utterly self-centered. He could be ruthless with people in the agency without even being aware of it. But for those who were in the royal favor, he was all charm and they adored him."

Andrew's tone was gentle. "But why now, Molly?"

"It was simply the final straw—when Poppa refused to make a will including the children. In the early years, when he wouldn't adopt them, I had felt a terrible bitterness against him, but I knew it was no use to push him beyond a certain point.

"For years he wanted to have a child of his own. It was a matter of pride with him. It wasn't that he was so crazy about children—he wanted to produce his *own* child. We both went to doctors and finally they told me that it was Poppa whose fertility was too low to make it very likely that we would have a child. But I never told him because it would have been too devastating to his ego, so I let him believe the problem was with me. That's why I was surprised when Odette announced that he did have a child of his own. Then the inspector told me yesterday that the blood tests ruled that out."

"Then," I asked, "who *was* Marie's father?"

"I've wondered about that too, Jane. Poppa told me Odette had been running around with other men before she left him. I suspect she didn't really know which was the father. When Odette told Poppa on the phone that the child was his, I think he just blocked out any doubts because he wanted it to be true.

"In any case, as the years went on, I stopped worrying about the adoption. I felt that because Poppa was so much older than I, he would probably go first, and since he had no other heir, everything would come to me. But now something has happened to change all that."

Andrew put his hand over Molly's. "I know, Molly. Before dinner I called Los Angeles and talked to your Dr. McLaren. At first he didn't want to tell me anything, but finally he admitted the truth. I'm so sorry. When did you first know?"

"Just two weeks before we came here. I went in for the regular checkup, and the chest X rays showed the cancer in both lungs—inoperable, as he probably told you. I wanted to wait until after this week before telling Poppa and the children. No use spoiling the cruise for everybody. Fortunately, lung cancer develops rapidly and doesn't cause much pain until the end. Other kinds are much worse, so I am lucky in that way. The doctor says I can buy some time with chemotherapy, but I'm not sure that I will do that now."

I looked up, blinking back tears. "I'm so sorry, Molly."

Andrew said quietly, "There's something I'm wondering about, Molly. When you believed that Poppa had a child by Odette, then the knowledge of your own—er, illness—would change all the expectations about the inheritance, since Poppa would probably—"

"Yes, dear, outlive me."

"Exactly. But, Molly, when Poppa finally learned the truth about you, wouldn't he then have made a will as you wanted him to do?"

Molly laughed with a bitterness that pierced me to the heart. "Yes, I'm sure he would. And then he would have destroyed it after I died or simply made a later one which would negate the first one. I have every reason to believe that, and I think you may have guessed why.''

Andrew looked at her sorrowfully. ''Yes, I think I have. That was what first made me suspect the truth. When Jane described going down to your cabin that day to get the magazine and Poppa was on the phone, I wondered then, but nothing clicked until this evening.''

''Yes, that was it.''

''I understand now,'' I said. ''Poppa was talking to Harry, and he told him to tear up something. Then he saw you and said something like, 'About that contract, Harry, just tear it up.' ''

''Yes.'' Molly's eyes kindled. ''But I knew what he meant. He was telling Harry to tear up the letter I had mailed to him, the one containing the will. I saw the guilty look on his face when we walked in the door. He tried to make it sound as if he had been talking about a contract, but I knew better. At that moment I felt such a fury that I simply shook all over. When I poured out his wine and he said he would take his medicine later, I knew he was planning to call Harry back as soon as I left to make sure he would destroy the envelope addressed in my handwriting. I laid his two tablets on the table and dropped several more into his glass. I was sure he would drink it off in a single gulp, as he usually did, and never notice a thing.

''Of course, I was right about Poppa's conversation with Harry. The next day, when I got back to the boat, after I had been hurt, and after—after Poppa was gone, I called Harry. He had already heard about Poppa's death from Don, and he said he was not too surprised—he thought Poppa was a pretty sick man.

''Then I asked if Poppa had told him to tear up a

letter addressed in my handwriting, and he said yes. So, I said, when the letter arrived, he was to keep it after all—that it was very important and Poppa had changed his mind about it before he died."

Andrew nodded. "So the will Poppa made will be valid?"

"Yes. Now that we know the girl Marie isn't his daughter after all, he has no other relatives. In that case, his estate would have come to me eventually, but with the will, things will move much faster."

Molly stood up and walked to the window and back. "There's something I want you both to understand. It wasn't only the money for the children that I cared about. It was Poppa's lack of feeling. I felt betrayed. They were such sweet children, affectionate and loving to him, but because they were not his own flesh and blood he never truly loved them."

Molly sat down again. "Of course I thought that his taking the medicine would appear to be an accident. If I hadn't been attacked and sent to the hospital, I would have washed out the glass when I got back to the boat that evening, not really imagining it would matter, but just routinely tidying up. I was horrified when the police began questioning everyone, especially when Don and Ellen seemed to fall under suspicion."

We sat in silence for a moment. Then Molly sighed. "There is something else I want to say which may help you to understand. There was an element of pity in what I did. Ever since Poppa's second heart attack, he had been getting weaker and was going downhill pretty rapidly."

Andrew nodded. "That's what Rosanna said to me, that she thought he was much sicker than other people realized."

"Yes. She was right. For Poppa to consent to rest every afternoon and go to bed early was unheard of.

He had to be really sick to agree to such a program. He could hold up for a few hours at a time and seem to be his old self, but I knew the effort it cost him. For a long time I had worried about what would happen if I weren't there to look after him. Then when I found out about the cancer, I had often wished that he would be taken soon, before me.

"This may sound inconsistent, and it is. You see, in one way I felt a lot of bitterness toward him, but on the other hand, after all our years together, I was fond of him. I knew how much he hated being sick and how he relied on me like a child with its mother, and I felt a tremendous compassion for him. This is not an excuse for what I did, because if I had not been seized with fury at that moment I would never have actually done it. But it does mean that I don't feel the kind of remorse that I would otherwise suffer. He was an old and dying man, with a lot of pain before him, especially today, when doctors can prolong life whether it's viable or not. What I did was wrong, but I can't be sorry he's been spared all that. My only concern now is that I don't want the children to know, at least until after—after I'm gone. Jane, dear, will you be the one to tell Ellen and she in turn can tell Don?"

"Of course, Molly. But I'm sure they will understand if you tell them now."

For the first time, tears spilled from Molly's eyes. "I know it's cowardly, Jane, but I simply can't do it. It's going to be a difficult time for Don and Ellen at best. I know in their hearts they will forgive me. I simply can't talk about it. Do you understand, dear?"

I nodded and kissed her cheek.

"And Andrew," Molly went on, "I have a commission for you, too, if you are willing. When I first learned that the police suspected murder, I immediately wrote this out in case anything should happen to me and someone else should be accused.''

She handed Andrew a sealed envelope. "Will you please put this in your safe deposit box when you get home? It tells the whole story. And then—afterward—you may tell your friend the inspector. He will have to decide what action to take then. I hope it can be done without too much publicity.''

Andrew fingered the envelope Molly had given him. ''I know he'll do his best, Molly. As you know, he has no specific evidence against Odette, but this will be a safeguard against anyone being falsely accused.''

I hesitated, then spoke up. ''I have a little request. When the time comes, I'd like to tell Marie that her mother was not guilty of Poppa's murder. It wouldn't be necessary to mention your name, Molly—she would take my word for it, I'm sure.''

''Yes, of course, Jane, please do.''

Andrew stirred. ''What really bothers me is that Odette undoubtedly did commit two of the crimes. She certainly attacked you, Molly. She had learned the correct details of the will from Marie and quickly saw that with you out of the way, Poppa's money would go directly to his heirs. Of course, she had no idea that blood tests would rule out his paternity. It also seems to me quite certain that she was the one who pushed Poppa into the canal. She knew he couldn't swim, and I think she intended him to drown, just as I believe that she meant for you to die. We can never prove any of this, but I believe she thought you were dead when she left you. I wish there were some way of bringing her to justice.''

Molly looked at Andrew with an ironic smile that wrung my heart. "Well, Andrew, you are quite illegally letting me get by with murder. I suppose it's only poetic justice that Odette should escape!''

29

Back in London, I sat with James in the tiny garden of our Bloomsbury flat. The afternoon sun, after a capricious day of hide-and-seek with rain clouds, had asserted itself, luring me onto the chaise longue in my shorts and sleeveless top. James sat on the postage-stamp lawn beside my chair, plying me with wine from one of the bottles I had brought from Burgundy.

"And that's the whole story," I said. I had talked to James on the phone several times during the cruise and afterward, giving the bare facts of what was going on. Now I had filled him in on all the details.

He looked at me reprovingly. "I am happy to say that as your solicitor, the information you have just given me is privileged."

"What on earth do you mean?"

"Hasn't it occurred to you, my lovely and erstwhile brainy wife, that you and Andrew are withholding vital information from the police in a murder case?"

"James! Do you seriously expect that we would turn Molly over to the French authorities so she could die in the Bastille, or whatever, instead of at home with her family? It's only for a short time, I'm afraid."

"Yes, darling, I do understand. I'm simply glad all this isn't happening in jolly old England!"

"I do see what you mean. Actually, Andrew is the one with the sticky problem, isn't he? Inspector Moreau is his friend. That makes it even more difficult not to tell him about Molly."

James thought for a moment. "I suspect that in some way he *will* tell him, quite informally and without offering any proof. You see, without Molly's confession, the inspector would have no more evidence against her than he had against Odette. And once Molly is back in the States, there is little he could do in any case in the brief time left."

As we talked on about the people involved in the events of the week, I reported the budding romance between Don and Julie.

"And they managed the whole thing without any help from my little matchmaker?" James teased. "What about the wife for Andrew you promised me?"

I smiled in what I hoped was a tantalizing manner.

James said, "You're looking frightfully smug."

"It's much too soon to be sure, but he and Ellen are very much attracted—"

"Oh, I say!" James looked genuinely pleased. "That would be splendid, wouldn't it?"

He refilled our glasses. "This *is* a marvelous wine, my love."

"I didn't think the budget would stand for a *grand cru*," I told him, "but this one is pretty close to paradise."

"Are you fishing for a line from the *Rubaiyat?*"

I sat up and kissed his ear. "No, darling, but even without the loaf of bread underneath the bough, I'd say we have paradise enow."